PENGUIN · SHORT · FICTION

"Not that the story need be long, but it will take a long while to make it short."
— Henry David Thoreau

Resident Alien

The author of five previous prize-winning books, Clark Blaise's stories and essays appear in over thirty anthologies. Born in North Dakota, educated at Denison University and the Writers' Workshop of the University of Iowa, he has taught in Montreal and Toronto, at Skidmore College, and in the Iowa Writers' Workshop.

Blaise was writer-in-residence at Emory University and is now at Columbia. Blaise is married to novelist Bharati Mukherjee and they have two sons.

RESIDENT ALIEN

Clark Blaise

*For Suniti
with respects
Clark Blaise
on a Toronto Street
17 Feb
'86*

Penguin Books

Penguin Books Canada Limited, 2801 John Street,
Markham, Ontario, Canada L3R 1B4
Penguin Books Ltd., Harmondsworth, Middlesex, England
Penguin Books, 40 West 23rd Street, New York, New York 10010 U.S.A.
Penguin Books Australia Ltd., Ringwood, Victoria, Australia
Penguin Books (N.Z.) Ltd., Private Bag, Takapuna, Auckland 9,
New Zealand

First published by Penguin Books Canada Ltd., 1986

Copyright © Clark Blaise, 1986
All rights reserved.
Typesetting by Jay Tee Graphics Ltd.
Manufactured in Canada

Canadian Cataloguing in Publication Data
Blaise, Clark, 1940-
Resident alien

ISBN 0-14-008234-4

I. Title.

PS8553.L34R47 1986   C813'.54   C85-099353-9
PR9199.3.B6R47 1986

Except in the United States of America, this book is
sold subject to the condition that it shall not, by way of
trade or otherwise, be lent, re-sold, hired out, or otherwise circulated without the publisher's prior consent in
any form of binding or cover other than that in which
it is published and without a similar condition
including this condition being imposed on the
subsequent purchaser.

To Bharati

Acknowledgements

Material in this book has appeared in numerous magazines, and in various forms. I wish to thank the editors for their permission to cut, rewrite and republish my work at this time.

Portions of "The Voice of Unhousement" appeared in *Canadian Literature* 100, *The North American Review*, *Saturday Night*, and *Books in Canada*.

Portions of the Introduction originally appeared as "Tenants of Unhousement" in *The Iowa Review*.

"South" was commissioned by the Canadian Broadcasting Corporation for its radio series "Anthology" and for reprinting in *Small Wonders*. Its first published appearance was in *Canadian Forum*.

"Identity" was published in *8: Best Canadian Stories*, John Metcalf and Leon Rooke, eds. (Ottawa: Oberon Press).

"North" was published in *Saturday Night* and republished in *New Press: Canadian Prize Stories*.

"Memories of Unhousement" was first published by *Salmagundi* and was reprinted in the *Pushcart Prize VIII* volume.

The author wishes to acknowledge the assistance of the Guggenheim Foundation and the National Endowment for the Arts during the writing of this book.

RESIDENT ALIEN

Contents

Introduction   1

Autobiographical Fragment:
    The Voice of Unhousement   7

The Porter/Carrier Stories:
    South   45
    Identity   59
    North   77
    Translation   107

Autobiographical Fragment:
    Memories of Unhousement   163

Introduction

Introduction

Sociologically, I am an American. Psychologically, a Canadian. Sentimentally, a Québécois. By marriage, part of the Third World. My passport says Canadian, but I was born in America; my legal status says immigrant. Resident Alien. Everywhere I see dualities. The continent of gringos, everything north of the Rio Grande, is sliced in half, and I occupy both sides, uneasily. My parents quartered that northern half between them: English and French, and all the silence that entails. I lived my childhood in the deep, segregated South, my adolescence in Pittsburgh, my manhood in Montreal, and have started my middle age somewhere in middle America. My father is dead, buried in New Hampshire in a plot called by the parish, "*le p'tzee kwang du Canado*"; my mother is in a nursing home in Winnipeg, unconscious of her name, her age, her very existence.

This book is a journey into my obsessions with self and place; not just the whoness and whatness of identity, but the *whereness* of who and what I am. I call it an autobiography in tales and essay, though it contains some of the most thoroughly invented stories I have ever written.

My earliest souvenirs, the ones that I've tried to preserve in some of these stories and memoirs, are of movement through the continent, the sense of living form that spoke to me through maps: my mother's atlases and *National Geographic*s and the folded maps my father stuffed in glove compartments that were entrusted to me on our endless moves. I spoke to my parents through maps because their silence was otherwise impenetrable; I saw their lives most clearly in the places they'd made their own. I achieved my own identity, such as it is, through the places I absorbed. If I have any distinction at all as an author, it is through acting out, dramatizing, the background setting of a conventional existence and teasing from it the stuff of nightmare and wonder.

I realize I have a passionate, and by that I mean erotic, relationship with the surface of the earth. Not just what's quaint or beautiful, but what's built upon, ruined and abandoned. I am a Peeping Tom of the Interstates and the Blue Highways; there is nothing more wonderful, more relaxing, more expectant to me than the interior of my car or a train or even a plane and the thought of just *moving*. Going somewhere, anywhere, for no special purpose. Time stands still, life is suspended, and if mystical union is possible in this life, I achieve it.

I have treated this continent promiscuously. I was divorced thirty times before the eighth grade, married briefly to Pittsburgh and Montreal after a morganatic relationship with central Florida and I have been divorced another twenty-five times since I married. I am the Bluebeard who has married only once.

> Clark Blaise
> Iowa City, Iowa
> October 1985

Autobiographical Fragment: The Voice of Unhousement

The Voice of Unhousement

The Voice of Unhousement

I have been trying to find the centre of my imagination. Where does the impulse come from, and why does the voice and shape and subject matter after twenty years remain the same? Why the first-person narrator, why the child and adolescent character, why the adult looking back? Why the relative silence on marriage and fatherhood, the scarcity of relationships, the elevation of the private and psychological over the social and political? Why am I wedded like a reborn Wordsworth to the epic of my own becoming, the origins of a calling, the hints of a talent? Why are most of my narrators themselves writers? I am like a dog tied to a post and then forgotten; I have sniffed every inch of my turf, I've dug it up, I've soiled it, I've hounded my life for meaning as though it were somehow prototypical, epic and exemplary, rather than sheltered, eccentric and utterly accidental.

I'm not a natural writer, not if I understand the

childhood of most authors. I was cut out to be something else, but I never discovered what it was. My childhood reading wasn't anything like a normal author's. I've read essays by Graham Greene, Forster, Sartre and Waugh; I've read Quentin Bell's biography of Virginia Woolf, Edel's biographies of Henry James and Gay Wilson Allen's of William James, and in all of them (and dozens more — I love literary biographies) I'm intimidated by what those children had already read by the age of eight or nine. "I suppose it was in my eighth summer, entranced by Gibbon . . . " or "My sisters and I performed little *commedia dell'arte* inspired indirectly by Juvenal . . . " Latin chronicles, the standard biographies, Shakespeare and the nineteenth-century French, English and Russian masters. They never wasted a minute trying to convince themselves they were normal. Did they fish, listen to baseball and football, stand in front of a radio taking their cuts with every reported pitch? In the rural Georgia and Florida schools that I first attended, an inclination to read might have revealed a reckless disregard for survival.

There was only one book in my life, at least up to the age of twelve, and that was the atlas. From it I typed out, at the age of seven and eight, a 120-page compilation of all the salient descriptive facts about the surface of the earth. By six I had known all the state and provincial capitals (thanks to maps my mother hung in the kitchens of those steamy subtropical apartments), and I would cut my meat and bite my graham crackers in the shapes of states and countries (one big bite from the corner of a double graham gives you an accurate Idaho); by seven I'd added the world capitals; by eight all the cities in the world (1930 census, alas) with over fifty thousand people; by nine I knew all the counties and their seats and by ten I had abandoned the atlas for world and country maps of my own creation, hand-painted with imaginary mountain ranges, cities and rivers, all very precisely named in languages of my own invention which borrowed heavily from Polish. I made up lists of new mountains and rivers and cities, and memorized *their* heights, lengths and populations.

Of course I think of it now as an artist's natural evolution from passionate but passive observation and unconscious mimicry, through to the creation of personal mythology. I was helpless before facts of any kind — I did the same with a handbook of Florida fishes, with my mother's old Canadian bird guides, with star charts, with baseball stats, car models, French, German and English monarchs, atomic weights and the periodic table.

The other book of my childhood and adolescence was the twelve-volume *Collier's Encyclopedia*, which I read through perhaps twice a year. I was told it contained everything known by man, which I must have considered advantageous to the omniphile I hoped to become. I was especially interested in calculating how old famous people had been when they died. I remember thinking that I, born in 1940, would probably live to see the next century, but that my parents, born in 1903 and 1905, would not — what does it do to a life, knowing that one century would totally contain it? I compared myself with others born in 1840 — would I be a burn-out before the century turned? Or should I wait, hold back my energies, until the new century released them? I was the kind of kid (I'm sure there are many) who was taken to his first movie in Atlanta in 1945 and shouted out, "What'll that company call itself in the year two thousand?" Already worrying about 20th Century Fox: such long-scale worries! Such belief in my immortality!

Even at eight or nine I could not imagine living a life that would not someday be glorified in the encyclopedia. This may be arrogance and ego; it may also be revenge on anonymity — on being, literally, a nobody, from nowhere.

The cataclysm in my life was my parents' divorce. Absurd, I know; it was the most predictable of occurrences, and it happened late enough in my life — nineteen — when all paternal obligations had been met. Yet, however calmly and maturely I took it, and however cordial and correct I remained with my father, I realize that I never accepted it, never forgave it, never really survived it. Their divorce formed a knot in my character; my life collapsed around it like a compacted star, and the density of that black hole will warp my work till I die.

I am comfortable with adolescent characters not because of a lack of interest in adults or inexperience in life, or attraction to the teenager *per se*, but because I am dependent on a world made explicable by my mismatched parents in their desperate marriage. So long as they are together, all things are possible. Their absurd incongruity calls up and somehow justifies the harshest and most beautiful images from my experience and out of my imagination. I write from an undisclosed adult perspective at a point in time after their break-up, looking back to a time before it happened, when the potential for divorce, the *logic* for divorce, the *imperative* for divorce, was temporarily set aside. Even when their divorce is not mentioned, it is the subtext, the precondition, the "big truth" behind the story.

Every writer has his or her own big truth: for Hemingway it was the nihilism of the Great War, for Faulkner, the sin of slavery, or Nabokov, the expulsion from Russia, or the Holocaust — a suppressed wound. The bigger the truth the better the fiction (alas); mine is the stuff of 90 percent of young people, unless enhanced. Life without my parents' unspoken, unacted, erotic violence is literally unimaginable to me, just as life *after* their divorce seems somehow absurd, lacking in pain, tolerance and moral authority.

I need the shelter of their marriage; their complications and polarities. They are the heavens and the landscape of my imagination, the indispensable maps leading north and south into Quebec and the Prairies and the Swamps, and even to Europe. To their Moral Atlas, I have added only India. They are endlessly available and compliant; they survive transmutation and still bounce back, pure and unknowable. They are the light source, the solar energy to my lunar self; they keep me not quite modern and combatively at odds with the meta-literatures and strenuous fabulations of an exhausted imagination. I want literature even now to teach me about life, not about itself.

That still does not explain the source of imagery, and for that I can only turn to water. Bodies of fresh water in Florida and Canada had a parenting effect on my imagination. I grew up on the wild shores of Lake Harris and Lake Griffin in central Florida, back in a time when they were utterly savage. Somehow, I ingested the sights and smells of putrescence, and of a primordial, unspoiled plenitude that has now vanished from the common experience, even of Floridians. Harry Crews in *A Childhood* and Frank Conroy in *Stop-Time* have written of it, but the home of all such imagery is probably Africa, Latin America and the Caribbean. We have seen a touch of the living prehistory of the planet and a triggering of the brain's own disremembered past.

It seemed that any casual, quiet moment by the shore

would yield encounters with every exuberant class of the vertebrate world: bird, fish, mammal and reptile, in no clear hierarchy of viciousness. All we were missing were piranha fish. When the sun penetrated the lake surface in a band of intense green light, I'd see monster bass, larger gar and 'gators and enormous softshell turtles drift across from the shadows. I knew the universe was teeming with monsters and that they were hidden, and I knew it from the age of six.

I remember even now a spectacle that belongs in Hieronymus Bosch. Dozens of mudfish nailed by their tails to cypress trees in front of a moss-picker's shanty. Those fish, their primitive lungs permitting life out of water for days at a time, whacking the trees with their heads, their air-bladders making Donald Duck noises, while sand-castle drippings of black mud built up under the propped-open mouths.

And so the images of the unconscious were planted early and privately by the peculiar wealth of southern poverty, and I grew to believe in the coexistence, or the simultaneity, of visible and occult worlds: duplicities, masks, hidden selves, discarded languages, altered names, things not being what they seemed. Add to that the continual moves — thirty before the eighth grade — the social adjustments to new schools and new cities every few months, the tension of my parents' marriage and the gifted memory and the ego-thrust towards immortal vengeance, and you have the formative, pre-literate experience of an eventual artist (if lucky), or a functional neurotic. It still took a series of fortunate accidents and gifted teachers to coax the writer from all that unformed, possibly poisonous sludge.

The Voice of Unhousement

I began to write from a desire to impress my experience — to avenge myself — on the blank understanding of my fellow undergraduates at Denison University. I had known a time and place in America — the deep South of the mid- to late forties — that was already history. I had been let out of school to watch Klan floggings and cross-burnings. I'd seen a lynching, or rather a post-lynching. I had attended segregated schools in a county 70 percent black, I had seen alligators and manatees, pumas, chain gangs, sharecroppers, moss-pickers, and I had attended school with morons and been doused with delousing powder and had my feet swabbed with carbolic acid for hookworms and my head shaved for ringworm.

In the beginning, then, I thought of myself purely as a southern writer on the basis of five potent years in my life — ages six through ten — spent in the swamplands and hamlets of north-central Florida. Faulkner was my guide: his language, his evocation of doom, of age, of the implacable determinants of race, class and history. My small world fit perfectly in the Yoknapatawpha legend; I had seen all the same types, gone to schools with them, spoken like them, seen the towns with their statues to the Confederate dead, been dismissed from school for Confederate Memorial Day and Jeff Davis's Birthday, and listened to my teachers' rapturous litanies on the sins, lineage, probable insanity and vile practices of the archvillain, Abraham Lincoln. We'd been given little Confederate flags at school so we could line the streets of Leesburg at night, cheering the unmasked parade of the Klan and the motorcade they led as it proceeded to Venetian Gardens, a doubleheader, and the crowning of the Watermelon Queen. Where are you now, Dolly Beard,

Watermelon Queen of 1948, senior at Leesburg High?

And like a child out of Faulkner I had roamed woods, fished, played and slumbered in the midst of a tropical torpor that was also a tropical maelstrom. I remember years, it seems now, of retiring to a screened-in porch with nothing but a Coke and the radio playing "The Game of the Day" from somewhere up north, but I also recall the furies of Florida: hurricanes, the scream of a mountain lion, the thrashing of a 'gator just under a rotten pier, the braiding of watermoccasins in my path. I remember the floating balls of squirming catfish larvae, and trying to break them up with a flick of my pole. I remember trailing an enormous woodpecker so deep into cypress swamps that I was knee-deep in warm water with no path out, and the bird — maybe a classifiably extinct ivory-billed, but probably an equally impressive pileated — was tapping above me while 'gators whistled nearby and deer could be heard plunging into deeper water that surrounded me.

I understood those favourite words of Faulkner, and I used them myself: *deep, beyond, further*. It was Faulkner, to his glory, the divine and sometimes tangled rhetorician, who had the faith and the tact to title a story simply and forever, "Was." It is a title for a collective experience of story-telling.

Those were a few of the realities I wanted to convey to my suburban-bred mid-western classmates at Denison University in the late fifties. I might look like them, sound like them, behave imperfectly like them, but I shared nothing of their experience, outlook, values or ambitions. For the first three or four years that I wrote, I considered myself nothing more than a southerner and, if the truth dare be told, nothing less than Faulkner's heir.

"Write what you know," the instructors teach, but the better instructors know that the process is far more devious than that. If we *know* it, chances are it's too boring to write. Grace Paley has amended the truism somewhat: "Write what you don't know about what you know," and that takes us back into Faulkner's dark caverns of beyond, deeper and ago. If we wrote only what we knew and showed and never told, our writing would be crippled of authority (emphasis on the first two syllables). What I *knew*, at the age of twenty, was suburban life in Pittsburgh in the mid-fifties; I knew it cold. I knew the retail trade in furniture, paper routes, baseball, the charms and terrors of women and gobs of facts in astronomy, sports, archaeology and geography. Those were the elements, in fact, of many later stories and my first novel, but if I had tried it as an undergraduate — and probably I did — it would have come out like warm, flat soda water.

It's alchemy, taking the facts, the common language, the world and characters we know, and transforming them into something never before seen, hitherto unknown and forever fresh. (Do you know what's wrong with that sentence? the Faulknerite in me asks. It's that last word, "fresh." Not wrong because of its meaning, but wrong because of its rhythm. "Never before seen" is a phrase of five syllables, as is "hitherto unknown," and I now must find a *two*-syllable synonym for "fresh" to balance the scales of "forever." But I also like the alliteration. Fragrant? Or a good Faulknerian "fecund"?) Forever fertile.

Denison has a professor of English, a poet and a great teacher of poets and fiction-writers by the name of Paul Bennett. He gave me a "B" in my senior year Advanced

Fiction class, so he's no push-over. He also gave me an "A-minus" in my first writing course in my sophomore year, when I was a struggling geology major, otherwise doing poorly. He has in common with all great handlers of young talent the qualities of faith and patience. Yes, he taught us to write what we knew about (to curb our natural propensity for second-hand fantasy) and to show, not tell, but he also emphasized trusting ourselves, cutting always deeper into our experience until the unknown in the face of the known lay revealed. Trust the story, let it take you over your head; drown a little, but remember to come back with what you saw. His patience rewarded me with a career: I wrote bad poems, bad character sketches (pure *Reader's Digest* stuff), bad stories about men in life rafts and western shoot-outs, and then one last story at the end of the course, a story called "Broward Dowdy," which excited him. It was the reason he taught: to see the emergence of talent, to be there when it started to happen. But I was still a geology student, and I thought I was going to transfer to Pitt — my parents had just started their divorce, and the money for an expensive school like Denison had dried up. But the divorce dragged on, and my father was solvent for one more year, and I returned to Denison as an English major and as a writing student. In the year remaining to me at Denison, I vowed to read a book every day; I started a book-reviewing column for the weekly paper, co-edited the two literary magazines on campus and published my stories and poems in them. Three years later, when I was married and living as a graduate student in Iowa, "Broward Dowdy" became my first story accepted by a national magazine, and I put it at the head of my second book of stories, fifteen years after writing it.

When I graduated in 1961, after winning the various campus writing prizes — which I also judged (this was in a politically innocent era) — with stories so swampy they should have been sprayed, I went on to the summer writing class of Bernard Malamud, at Harvard. I needed validation — Denison was fine, and Paul Bennett is a great man — *so far as they went*. The question was, how far did they go? There was only one way to find out, perilous as that way might be. There were hundreds of Denisons out there, and thousands of campus hotshots; but there was only one Malamud, one Harvard, and only ten places in his class.

The luckiest move in my writing life was the acceptance to Malamud's class. Malamud was coming to Harvard from Oregon, and the ten slots in his class were already chosen by readers in the Harvard English department. Who knows what criteria? — but Harvard and Harvard Square are never lacking for dozens of young Updikes and hundreds of young Thomas Wolfes, talents and egos abounding. Fortunately, I hadn't known the course was closed even before I'd sent in my deposit and my sample story. Fortunately, it was Bernard Malamud teaching and not some other eminence looking for a well-paid summer vacation in the heart of genteel academia. I went to the English office in Warren House, after hitch-hiking in from Pittsburgh.

"Oh, that course was closed weeks ago," the secretary told me.

"Is there a waiting list?" I asked. "I sent in my manuscript as soon as I heard Malamud was teaching —" I must have thought that even having heard of Malamud, let alone having read him from the heart of Baptist America, was evidence of sufficient grace to insure admission. To the two of us at Denison who had read Malamud, he was the greatest writer in America. I had never seen, let alone met, a "real" writer.

"You can go up and ask him," she suggested.

He's there? I can ask him? It was a different era. Those

of us from the provinces had never seen an author we truly admired. I was terrified, and I walked around Warren House so many times I was afraid he'd go home before I could rehearse my presentation. Finally I confronted myself: you borrowed a hundred dollars for the course. You hitched here. You have a friend in Belmont Hill who's putting you up. You've told yourself you're going to be a writer. Face him, you idiot. Your life is over, here and now, if you can't take this course.

This is your moment of truth, Blaise.

He was seated at the end of a long room. The bookcases were empty but for shoeboxes and stacks of manuscripts, thick bundles bitten by rubber bands. There were more stacks on his desk. He was not particularly smiling or welcoming. He said, "I asked them to send me the manuscripts in Oregon, but instead they made the selections. That's not fair to the people who submitted in good faith. Find yours up there and give it to me."

"It's just this story," I said — I'd brought a second copy, razored from our Denison campus magazine. The catalogue hadn't mentioned thousand-page novels as a minimum consideration. "Come to the first class tomorrow, Blaise. I can't promise you're in, only that I'll read it."

I wrote two more very southern stories for that class. All that Malamud had seen of my work, in fact, were stories with such heavy southern dialogue that I felt absurd reading them aloud in class. There was something of an imposture about me; feeling myself Canadian more than American (the divorce had opened up the floodgates of an urgent nostalgia; I was hitch-hiking on all long week-ends up to Quebec City from Belmont Hill), and obviously sounding like any other college-bred easterner. I was writing scenes that Erskine Caldwell would shun. And the class was, as expected, bright, ambitious and accomplished (at least four others that I'm aware of have gone on to establish writing careers). I was a little embarrassed by my material in that Ivy League, half high-WASP, half Jewish setting, and I felt the disapproval of my classmates, if not of the teacher. It's so easy to appear the buffoon when you follow your illiterate young characters down a swamp on a gar hunt, or when idiot brother rapes nympho sister while out gigging frogs. My classmates were writing *European*-set stories, love-affair stories, abortion stories, even Africa stories, and many of them were submitting *chapters*. Or they were turning out high-powered intellectual farces and fantasies that echoed Barth and prefigured Pynchon, Heller and Vonnegut. The big book of those in the know was Gaddis's *The Recognitions*. Harvard was the big time, all right; the overflow of the next ten rejectees from Malamud's course was being taught by John Hawkes, just down the hall. At Malamud's prompting, I read *The Lime Twig*, and everything earlier. So: it was possible to keep the rhythms of Faulkner, the rhetoric and incantations of voice, and get rid of that inauthentic southern material. I rejoiced.

That was the terror I faced. I wanted to write, and life itself had given me a boost by smearing me in the paste of a memorable southern childhood. But it was an accident. Those memories were a shopping list, and I was quickly exhausting the menu of available experience. Then what? Be a Pittsburgh suburbanite? And so I wrote one very strange story for Malamud that summer: an over-ambitious, incomprehensible (also Faulknerian) monologue of a senile Canadian doctor, remembering and living (in his hospital bed) his heroic service during the influenza epidemic of 1919, while (in searing irony!) he is really an eighty-five-year-old whimpering husk soiling his sheets in a Winnipeg hospital. My grandfather, obviously. At the very least, it was a change of material, though of course (as Malamud pointed out), I had scrambled a good story and a strong character for the dubious pleasures of sophomoric experimentation. Of all the things to lift from Faulkner, I had to choose the Benjy monologue.

Malamud's instructions are as simple as the universal reader demands and as complicated as the most ambitious author expects: focus on character, make every act, every detail, dramatic. Fiction dramatizes the multifarious adventures of the human heart — advice that we young Barthists (we'd all read *The Sot-Weed Factor* and *The End of the Road*) and Gaddisites probably associated with the death of literature. That was Dickensian! We wanted the clean lines and sharp edges of modernism; we'd been raised on irony, juxtaposition and every conceivable complication of structure. On days when we didn't provide stories of our own, Malamud introduced us to Isaac Babel, Flannery O'Connor, Hemingway, James, Moravia. He read us stories — well-received ones by nameless contemporaries — and asked us to think twice before admiring such clever tricks, such facile manipulations. If a name was mentioned in class, by teacher or student, that I hadn't read — a simple enough event in those days, despite the two years of book-a-day reading — I'd have it read twice before the next class.

The mentors that last in our lives are those who do not press a case, do not try to shape, or inflate; do not lust for miniatures of themselves or even try to leave much of an impression at all. They are anything but charismatic; they teach by their tolerance and their conviction. They are calm, even serene, in the reconciliation of tolerance and authority; and, I think, they have one other great quality. Malamud and Bennett, as readers, as teachers and as writers, take *delight*; there is no other way of putting it. It was possible to *delight* these men, to see their eyes, mouth, brow suddenly dance over a sentence, a word, an idea. Oh, it is possible to enrage a teacher, to infuriate or to embitter him or her, but only the rarest, I think, instruct by an almost private show of delight.

When the summer school ended and Malamud went on to begin his career at Bennington (odd to think he was forty-seven that summer, so old and powerful and socketed in eternity to me at the time, and how quickly I'm closing on that age now), I stayed back in Boston, getting a job in a bookstore and taking an apartment with one of the wilder members of the summer class. I stayed with the job all winter, thinking I could remain out of university and somehow in the flow of that thing called "life," working just enough hours to finance my writing. As for living, I'd leave that to my apartment-mate. I hitched up to Bennington to visit Malamud one week-end; he came down to Harvard one afternoon while I was working, found the stack of his recently issued novel, *A New Life*, signed them, and, as the manager came running over, pointed to the books and said, "A deposit on Blaise's freedom for the afternoon. Let's beat it." And there I was, on a cool fall day in Harvard Square, walking with the writer I most admired (and still do), answering as best I could *his* questions about me: what did I intend to do with my life? Was I working? Was I happy? What could he do to help?

I do remember, one evening after work in the bookstore, slipping into the Lamont Library, taking out a new notebook and writing a story, "How I Became a Jew," that was literally a transitional story between South and North, as well as a tribute to Malamud. In one sitting; shades of Thomas Wolfe! I had started a novel, "The French and Jewish War," about my parents and I suppose about myself and twisted loyalties, and most of it was set in Canada. I would be writing it a year later, in Iowa, after the most momentous year in my life. I vomited the night on Dubuque Street in Iowa City when I read through those two hundred typed yellow pages with the big inked number at the top of every page (my God, *me*, at one hundred! At two hundred!!) and then unclipped the pages from the binder I had bought at the Harvard Co-op on the first day of Malamud's class, marched outside in the cold, lifted the lid of my garbage can and ripped the pages into shreds.

In February, 1962, I entered the Writers' Workshop. My first night in town, Paul Engle, the Director, invited me up for drinks. His other guest was Bharati Mukherjee, the writer from Calcutta. Miss Mukherjee was dazzling in a sari: poised, non-drinking, very British. I can't remember if we talked at all. One no more spoke to Miss Mukherjee than one spray-painted the Taj Mahal. She was so formal, so proper, so beautiful, I thought of her name as Miss Missmukherjee.

I knew nothing of India, cared little for it, and settled in for a long Iowa winter of serious writing on little money. Philip Roth was my teacher, and the classes contained some of the serious fiction writers, particularly short story writers, of the next two decades, like Raymond Carver, Andre Dubus, Phil O'Connor, John Yount, Joy Williams, Jim Crumley, Ted Weesner, Mark Costello, Paul Friedman, Dave Godfrey and Frank Chin. The poets were Mark Strand, Charles Wright, Marvin Bell and Jim Tate.

There was talent and ambition and pretension, too, all in outsize batches. And despair. We were the Iowa generation immediately before the Golden Era of John Irving and Tom McHale, Asa Babar and Nicholas Meyer, just before the time when New York agents and editors and California producers started breaking their bicoastal journeys in Iowa City in order to sign on new talent. Ours were still the literary-quarterly years, the years of reading the small magazines and shaping our stories to *Shenandoah's* needs, when fiction writers envied poets their relative fame and income. I remember a night in Kenny's Bar, when Paul Friedman said the best writer in America was a philosophy professor at Purdue, and Ray Carver countered that *he* knew the best: a medievalist at Chico State. William Gass and John Gardner had not yet published their first books. Four years later, workshop *students* had three-book contracts and six-figure paperback deals. To have been a mediocre talent in those years must have been humiliating.

But in 1962 it was still a quiet time of deep cold and serious ambition, when all the world was writing and all your friends were as good or maybe better than you were, and you couldn't afford to let up a minute. I remember summer nights in Iowa City, taking a walk at three A.M. in the eighty-five degree heat, and hearing the flood of language chatter from attic typewriters, and I would cut the walk short, go back to my own apartment and work till dawn. All those thousands of pages! Lost! Awful!! What madness was it?

And I remember a night in Iowa in 1963 in the early fall just weeks after I'd married Miss Mukherjee, walking down to the post office to send off yet another rejectable story to the *New Yorker* — in Iowa, a finished story could not languish even five minutes on your desk, no matter what the hour; the world would not forgive the delay! — and having it come to me that crazy as they are, *these* are the happy years in my life, when everything I write is perceptibly better than the thing before, when no one expects anything from me, when my future is unformed and I cannot say where I will be in a year's time and I can afford to sneer at the inevitable rejection slip that will greet this story, and the next and the next, and say to my friends in the bar, *it tells more about them than it does about me*.

I had arrived in Iowa in the winter of 1962; I went to Europe that summer, came back in the fall with an assistantship, married Miss Mukherjee a year later, became a father in the summer of 1964 and left for my first real teaching job, in Milwaukee, in the late summer of 1964 with a wife and son. We were twenty-four.

I remember nights in Milwaukee, parked in my new VW van, radio on, waiting for Bharati to be finished at Marquette. One station came through loud and clear, from a thousand miles away. It was the CBC station in Winnipeg, and I could hear my cousin Lynn conducting the arts interviews, and I could hear that exhaustive ten-minute province-wide weather report, utterly unchanged from my childhood and visits over the years, beginning with highs and lows that could chill the open hearths of Pittsburgh, wind and snow conditions first for "Winnipeg, Carman and Gimli" (which could be horrendous enough, in January), but leading to figures that were barely credible outside of laboratory conditions as the report marched ever northward. And still that silken voice, that dauntless wave of electronic imperturbability (could anyone imagine an American announcer not breaking in with a "get out them longjohns, Churchill, she's hitting fifty below tonight!") led on to areas of perma-dark, where herds of musk-oxen shouldered the wind: Moose Factory, Norway House, Pickerel Lake and, finally, "the Territories." Fifty-five below. Sixty below.

As always in my life, there was something behind me to help establish perspective. Milwaukee could be cold, wet and uncomfortable. But I came from the stock of heroic skaters on both sides (even if I failed them). My mother had walked to school one day in North Battleford, Saskatchewan, at sixty-three below. Down in musty Florida, she'd told me the story of walking on crusty snow that sounded like avalanches, of flinching from footsteps two blocks away, of tasting blood down her throat as capillaries exploded. I had stood at recess in my first Canadian winter, the boy just arrived from Florida, watching my classmates play broom hockey at forty below. Bright, confident, assertive, informed people, like my cousin and her parents, like my mother. And dark, self-destructive, violent sociopaths like my father, to give my character a tinge of treachery, glamour, irresponsibility. Half in love with both tendencies, fearing that I was totally the child of Winnipeg, I prayed for deliverance from the direction of Quebec.

And as I sat in our first car, waiting for Bharati's Marquette lectures to end, I turned on the CBC to another voice. A professor in Montreal by the name of Sidney Lamb at Sir George Williams University was delivering a series of lectures that winter on Shakespeare. They were the annual CBC Lectures: nothing too specialized; on the other hand, nothing too compromised either. Given my ignorance of literature prior to about 1950, I was probably the general audience he had in mind.

In those days, for those susceptible to it, no greater flattery existed on this continent than the daily buttering by the CBC. It presumed an audience of educated, liberally inclined, culturally informed, world-conscious, locally curious, chatty and *deeply Canadian* (in the all-embracing and all-restrictive sense of Anglo- or Franco-Canadian) listeners. In short: me, my mother and everyone like us. Our projection of an idealized self-image, however it makes us wince, however we may wish to parody it. I have lived my Canadian life in Montreal, Toronto and Winnipeg, among CBC types. The projection is true and false, expansive and restrictive, in just about equal doses. I was a rootless, deprived Canadian listening in Milwaukee to Sidney Lamb recording from studios on Dorchester Street in Montreal, relayed over my old hometown station, CBW, the only counterweight to KDKA in Pittsburgh in my life. I could hear Montreal and Winnipeg and Culture in his voice. All Canadians seemed to have that effortless Lorne Greene radio voice, a race of announcers, facile articulators.

I longed for those broadcasts. Sitting in the cold van in Milwaukee, I ingested the subtext of Sid Lamb's talk: somewhere, it said, this kind of stuff isn't even considered terribly highbrow. The CBC smugly assumes that enough cultural fragments still exist out there to justify such a commission. Somewhere in the corporate bosom lingers a cherished image of loggers, lawyers, fishermen and shopkeepers, students and housewives, pensioners — all clustered around a radio, in 1964! Saying *by cracky*! to a learned professor's chats on Shakespeare. Well, it moved me. It spoke (as Canada always spoke to me) of continuity, assured values, a unified voice. Canadians might laugh at that; they should, for it is only the mellow voice of a gawky youth, like those high-school boys who boast impressively deep radio voices while the rest of their hormones run them frail and ragged.

I had to have Montreal.

That was 1965, the year for young academics of the expanding universal market-place. By that time I had published six stories in obscure quarterlies, the point at which I had arbitrarily promised myself to get an agent, carry myself as a writer and unapologetically describe myself as one. Universities were knocking on our quonset hut. But Bharati and I had our applications out to Montreal. My imperialism, totally. She was happy in America, anywhere in America except the South would have done. But she was also a wife and mother: Indian wife, and mother — she submitted to my dream, or to my pitch. I was offered jobs by letter and by phone call, in Washington, Oregon and half the new campuses in California. But I was an east-coaster; people out there — how did they live? I'd only once been west of Omaha. I'd had it with America — its politics, its shallowness, its reaction, its disarray. But again McGill rejected me. *Tamarack Review* took my first quasi-Canadian story. *Prism*, out in Vancouver, took another. I was coming north.

But McGill leaped at Bharati, and so it was settled. She would teach and I would write, teaching English as a second language for McGill extension at night. The jobs I had turned down on the West Coast were for assistant professorships at eight and nine thousand dollars a year, three sections, two of them writing. Bharati would be earning the equivalent of six thousand dollars for four sections of freshman English, as a lecturer.

In June 1966, my son and I entered at Windsor with a vanful of furniture. Bharati stayed back to take her comps. I remember it as a glorious summer day, the fulfilment of my life to that time. I was admitted to the country of my parents' citizenship as a temporary worker on the basis of my McGill evening job, not on Bharati's appointment. Married women had no files of their own. I drove that thirteen hours to Montreal without a break, pumped by a new adrenalin.

Here, I believed, I would find my voice. Farewell, those swampy southern stories of my remote accidental past! Here, French and English as I was — here, remembering my brief Winnipeg childhood, my summers in Quebec and two adolescent summers in Brockville — *here*, I would take my place. This is where all my instincts had come from, where the agony of my life was merely a national allegory, where psychologically I was at home. By some Herculean effort and by some Odyssean restraint, I had managed to realign my life, lift myself back on the tracks I'd been derailed from twenty-five years earlier. Never had a thing seemed so right. Never had I behaved so passionately. I had the feeling that my American life was over; nothing from it counted. It would be like Quebec City all over again, but in English, with French all around us in the background.

The amazing thing is, it worked.

Thirteen years is the longest, by far, that I have lived in a single place; Montreal will remain my city for life. Predictably enough, the city did take the place of my warring parents — Montreal *is* my parents; I am once again their baffled son in its presence. I worked for both Neil Compton and Sidney Lamb. I heard my own voice pumped out over the CBC. Later, in Toronto, I sat one night at Massey College high table beside Northrop Frye, across from Marshall McLuhan. In Canada election to Olympus is possible. The myths have touched me. I met my whole generation of Canadian writers and aged with them; I was there when the exiles returned, I got to know the others before they passed away. I started a writing program in Montreal and taught in others in Toronto and British Columbia and Saskatchewan; I think I did find the next generation of talent, in classrooms or through the mails, and with John Metcalf I edited four books of "the best" in Canadian stories. More of my stories have been anthologized than I ever thought possible, from my Iowa origins. And it all started by joining a group, The Montreal Story-Tellers, the only conscious *gathering* of English-language prose writers in Montreal this century.

I was still discovering the city, or, more precisely, discovering parts of myself opened up by the city. I was respectful if not worshipful of all its institutions. I defended its quirks and inconsistencies as though defending myself against abuse; I was even charmed by things I would have petitioned against in Milwaukee, like separate Catholic and Protestant schools, Sunday closings, male-only bars (not only bars: McGill even barred its faculty club to female professors — something about the presence of females inhibiting the accustomed conversational saltiness of its warhorse membership). "The Frencher the Better" was my motto to cover any encroachment on the aboriginal rights of the English.

I was writing very openly, in the late sixties, of Montreal. The city was drenched with significance for me — it was one of those perfect times when every block I walked yielded an image, when images clustered with their own internal logic into insistent stories. A new kind of unforced, virtually transcribed story (new for me, at least) was begging to be written — stories like (from my first two books) "A Class of New Canadians," "Eyes," "I'm Dreaming of Rocket Richard," "He Raises Me Up," "Among the Dead," "Words for the Winter," "Extractions and Contractions," "Going to India" and "At the Lake" were all written in one sitting, practically without revision. I'd never been so open to story, so avid for context. I was reading all the Canadian literature I could get my hands on, reading Canadian exclusively; there was half a silent continent out there for me to discover.

In late 1970, under the guidance of British-born John Metcalf and native-Torontonian Hugh Hood, we — Hood and Metcalf, the Maritimers Ray Fraser and Ray Smith, and myself — became the Montreal Story-Tellers. The Story-Tellers is yet another instance of synchronicity and serendipity at work; contemporary Canadian literature was just being born, and we were in a time and place and possessed with the vision and commitment to assist the delivery.

Our purpose was admirably eleemosynary. We would charge two hundred dollars a performance — forty dollars apiece. Twice the amount paid by august quarterlies like *Fiddlehead* for my stories "Eyes" and "A Class of New Canadians." The Protestant school board wouldn't have us (I had assumed, until reading the full account in Metcalf's memoirs of these same years, "Telling Tales" in *Kicking Against the Pricks*, that the Protestants had rejected us because Hugh Hood is and was so relentlessly Catholic). But the island of Montreal is even richer in

Catholic schools, and the English Catholics, along with the off-island Protestants, were agreeable to trying us out.

Money, then, was the first goal. Hugh, as a matter of principle (everything with Hugh is a matter of principle) insists on top dollar for any creative work. John and the two Rays were living hand to mouth as free-lancers. Ray Fraser epitomized the word, and precarious consequences, of "freelancing." He raised it to an art while writing Fraseresque stories for the local tabloid, *Midnight*, in the unedited Maritime tall-tale tradition, touched with a bit of the Montreal macabre. DAD RAPES INFANT SON, SERVES HIM IN STEW.

Our second goal was a bit more combative. John was tired of the bloody poets getting all the readings and recognition. It seemed to us that the league of warblers had enjoyed their monopoly on the stages of the country quite long enough. Prose was intrinsically more interesting and easier to follow than poetry. There was no reason why stories, if limited to fifteen minutes (multiplied by five) should not move, delight and instruct any audience — and still not betray our own literary standards. This, it seemed to me, was a battle worth joining.

The third and most altruistic goal was to prove something to and for Canada. John had taught in the high schools and knew the attitudes of the boards and most of the teachers. Chesterton and Kipling as moderns, Morley Callaghan and Hugh Garner thrown in so the students could thrill to seeing the word "Toronto" in print. Just think what *we* could do: living, young, funny, sexy, bold, dirty, *Montreal* writers. We'd begin the great reaming-out, the great scouring of all those corroded cultural pipes. We'd have the rarest of all literary privileges — that of creating our own audience.

I remember those drives through unfamiliar but very Catholic parts of the island — a jolly band of prose troubadours in my car, or Hugh's. We were a hit from the beginning; I couldn't understand it. The bookings were coming three and sometimes four times a week. Every now and then I'd wince at our collective arrogance, inflicting all this shameless puffery, this elevating slobber, on immigrant youngsters whose English needs were for something more rudimentary and whose experiences of any literature was utterly virginal. (I am speaking of a past now, as remote as my swampy Florida childhood, when Asian and European immigrants were allowed to choose an English, not a French, education.) Then, a minute later, after applause, smiles, laughter, I'd think what a splendid, noble thing we were doing. Those kids were our perfect audience, uncorrupted by ghastly good taste, analogues to our purest intentions. Didn't we want to communicate the real, the actual, the tangible *montréalitude*? Didn't we want to present ourselves as serious writers who were also living, imperfect Montreal presences? Didn't we pride ourselves on the accessibility of our stories, that anyone could appreciate them? Our proudest boast was that — unlike Chesterton or Belloc or whoever-the-hell — *we were in the phone book*! Look us up, call us, talk to us. We drink, we fart, we get horny, we make fools of ourselves, our lives are usually in a mess, we're afraid of cops and taxes, and unlike the poseurs of an earlier time, we're not afraid to show it. Like kindergarten kids with finger paints, we wallow in it! We make art of it!

In a typical reading, repeated maybe sixty times in a three-year period, John and I did two voices from a segment of his novel, *Going Down Slow*, wherein a high-school teacher is so rude, drunk and honest that he gets thrown out of a sleazy folk-and-blues bar. Not the high-school teachers they were accustomed to. I then read about a man who watches Greek butchers in Outremont (my neighbours at the time) popping calf testicles into their mouths and sucking. Big Ray Smith read a chapter from *Lord Nelson Tavern*, a monologue on the pathos of being a tall girl in the cutesie-pie fifties and the revenge the girl extracts a few years later, and he read with such conviction that he ended up in tears while the audience laughed. Hugh's "Socks" (sometimes he read its accompaniment, "Boots") was about an immigrant from southern Italy who ends up working snow removal in wet socks; it was not a comedy, but it captured a world they knew. And there was Ray Fraser's unpredictable and never-repeated routine (he could write them in the car), tall tales of mounting disgust, teetering over a pit (one suspected) of imminent intervention from a hardly amused school hierarchy, often priestly.

Despite all that (and, of course, because of it) we became legitimate. We grew out of the ghetto of Catholic schools to the junior colleges and the university classrooms. We were featured in the second issue of the *Journal of Canadian Fiction* (my two tall tales in that issue, "Is Oakland Drowning?" and "The Voice of the Elephant," were inspired purely by our ensemble readings, the need for levity, brevity, and surreality. I wanted to be as precise as Metcalf, as witty as Smith, as various as Hood, as irreverent as Fraser). We read at the conventions of Protestant teachers. We popped up in Fredericton, Saint John and Ottawa. We got to be polished, convincing and even successful in all three of our initial goals. The stories we read aloud now appear, dozens of times, in the various new anthologies that exploded on the Canadian scene in the seventies.

The Story-Tellers is now a chapter in Canadian literary history. We're too grey and cranky to give collective readings any more. The easy work — the fire and passion — is behind us, but I have to feel the best work is still to come. For me, the years from the mid-sixties to the late seventies in Montreal were the public manifestation of an inner maturing. I learned in the group that I still needed an ensemble; despite my immodest flights of fancy, I wasn't yet ready to stand alone. I always had the sense that of the five of us, I was the one the audience hadn't heard of, and I was the one they had to endure after the famous Hugh Hood and the sexy Ray Smith and the satiric John Metcalf and the wacko Ray Fraser. So I learned to tame myself, and to wait.

And what of my parents in those years? They got together one last time, in the months when I was courting Miss Mukherjee. They had zipped through Iowa City before we were married, heedless charmers it seemed, on their way to California. "Lee's Interiors" was my father's idea this time: Marin County his destination. A small decorating studio to be run by my mother, accessories to be selected by my father. "Personal follow-up," that was the key. A small, high-class operation; all sales by appointment only, from catalogues. They didn't need me to wish them luck; it stitched up the most painful hole in my life.

When I next heard from my mother, it was in a phone call from Winnipeg. They had returned to Pittsburgh, supposedly to pack their things for the long trip west, and she had given my father the slip. He was still waiting for her in the ghastly rooming house she'd found him in, and she was not coming back. Could I go to Pittsburgh, tell him and bring the car back to Chicago? She was with her family — my grandmother, gradually losing her faculties, and her sisters. They had found her an apartment. They had reactivated her Manitoba licence. She'd be teaching in the fall.

All of this was a heavy burden to relate to an Indian wife, impeccably Brahmin, whose parents had been asking for my horoscope and who'd been waiting in vain for a description of my father's status, his income, his undoubted influence in the American economy (in India, my father-in-law had intervened in a potential love-match between his youngest daughter and the son of the local maharaja: maharajas were too low caste). Her father had wanted to know the quality of breeding that had been introduced to a family that had sprung directly from the knee of God.

I made the trip to Pittsburgh to pick up my mother's car, to load up her goods from her boarding house and to meet her in Chicago with them. My father came to his boarding-house door. It was a half-way house for broken, deserted, drunken, unemployed men, five of them between thirty and sixty, all down on their luck and money. My father, "Frenchie," did the cooking. There were open bottles of Scotch in his room, beer cans lining the hall; the clothes stank, the air was blue with cigarette smoke, the thermostat on high, the windows sealed. They were men who sought enclosures.

My father, who'd been the handsome one all his life, the "perfect specimen" in the words of doctors and admiring women, showed all his years now, and the battering of his plans. He'd been bested in mortal combat. My mother, and his ability to convince her of his sincerity after a brutal divorce and sleazy remarriage, had been his ticket back. His grey hair was now white. His ears seemed larger. He'd grown a moustache: a bar of white bristles. He met me in his pyjamas and bathrobe. He had only two wardrobes: silk suits, white shirts, gold (lots of gold) accessories, polished black shoes, gartered black silk hose. Or slippers, pyjamas and a silk robe. In his mind, if I understand it, there were only forward speeds and no reverse. It was all sales or seduction, an elaborate formality or a contrived intimacy. The real man, my father, I never met. I never talked to him. I never heard him speak to me except, I think, in one sentence.

He poured himself a drink. He poured me a drink. He assumed, properly, that some time in the last three years I'd grown up. I was married, soon to be a father. He'd seen Bharati, been charming — his charming, singing, French best — to her. He didn't ask me now how I'd found him, or what my mother had said about him. He was the sort of dapper man who lit his cigarettes immediately before leaving the house, before meeting a customer; to be seen in public without a fresh cigarette, to shake hands without first having to transfer the cigarette to the left hand, was to be seen unguarded, unprepared. He was a salesman, and he needed a product, or a prop, or else he was silent.

In a way, it's impossible to write this in any way but memoir; fiction would pull me into faint postures of amazement, even of admiration for the savage decisiveness of his life, the jaunty, breezy indifference to the consequences of his lost, vain lust. And if you fill in the gaps, fictionally, with his public charm, and his hard-scrabble youth and the undeniable romantic edginess of his life in America, then sympathy would flow like credit. It's easy to endow him with higher motives, with *élan*, with some mysterious, potent life force.

As the obviously introspective, morally scrupulous, unconfident son of an earnest, progressive, upright mother, it was a legacy I wanted to claim. Myself as gipsy, as criminal, outcast.

I respond as well to a memory of my mother, one of those nights in my junior year of college when she was a prisoner in the only house we'd ever owned, in the hills south of Pittsburgh. My father was out with his woman; she would phone my mother every few hours, to taunt her. (After her mind started going, my mother turned paranoid. People in the apartment above her had ways of watching where she was standing. They would stand just over her and stamp their feet, hurl threats, mock her fears.) She pressed a *Reader's Digest* article on me. The title, more or less, was, "Are You Living with a Sociopath?" And in her secretive way she'd ticked off all seven danger signs. She'd underlined the operative descriptions. "Yes!" she'd written, and "Lee!" and "To a 'T'!"

She was right, it could have been a portrait of the man she married. Is he charming to strangers? *Yes!* Does he easily gain their confidence? Good God, *Digest*, what do you think a salesman *is*? Have you caught him in fabrications? She'd never detected him in an unguarded truth. She was forever hearing from customers and friends of his birth in a château outside Paris, of his arrival as a child with his wealthy, dying parents, his subsequent abandonment at their death, his Boston upbringing, the two years at Harvard before the Depression threw him out on the streets. Ah, the crash of '29 . . . well. His eyes would mist, his voice grow foggy. A burden to shoulder — he, of course, had to support a large family of enormously talented brothers and sisters. He gave up his dream of medical school and took over the management of a chain of furniture stores all over the East Coast. He put his many brothers through medical and law school, saw his sisters through music school. His work even took him all the way up to Montreal, if you can believe it (they speak — no, *try* to speak a little French up there, he'd joke), where he met his charming wife, daughter of one of the wealthiest men in Canada. *Who's Who* — you can look it up. Then he'd sing — "*La vie en rose*," often, or "Around the World" and, towards the end, when he was trying to get my mother back, "Are You Lonesome Tonight?"

Does he have a temper?

A violent temper?

Is he subject to moods, to violent shifts of mood for inexplicable reasons?

Does he retain friendships? Does he have a sense of loyalty? Does he have friends he can count on?

My father had cronies, no friends. Even his cronies would come to my mother and say, "Lee's very lucky he has you. He'd be a bum without you." Once our store was started in Pittsburgh, he asked me to spread the word among my high-school friends to come to us for any furniture. The parents faithfully responded, and my father jumped the prices. Once *borax*, always borax. Our banker told my mother even before their divorce, "Your husband frightens me." Our doctor said, "I treat him for arthritis, but that's not his problem. For that he needs a different kind of doctor, understand?"

For the twenty years of her marriage, she lived with thirty moves, insecurity, lies, rude, surly and unfaithful behaviour. The quiet companionship of marriage — shared interests, conversations, confidences, pride, understanding — these things were simply outside his competence. He worked obsessively hard; he paid bills, he fantasized enormous dreams of wealth. He feared more than anything the poor-house, yet when he died it required a contribution to the Society of the Precious Blood and a cheque from me to get him into that "little corner of Canada."

And yet, I want to say, I have cried rarely in these past twenty years. Once was on December 30, 1978, in Toronto when I got the news he had died. Another time was that night in Pittsburgh in his boarding house, the hall of coughs, when my father appeared, fresh cigarette lit, dressing-gown pleated over pyjamas, when he opened the door to his room, and collapsed on my shoulder. "I'm so lost, son, it's awful!" he cried, and for the first and maybe only time, I believed him.

The
Porter/Carrier Stories

South
Identity
North
Translation

South

South

It was the South. My father had been in an accident in Valdosta, and the word they used was *crushed*: his legs, his back, his ribs, his hip. His arms were merely broken. We had no insurance. Until the accident we had been surviving in town. I was in the second grade. My mother stayed in the three rooms that weren't quite an apartment but served the landlady as one. They were three equal-sized rooms, all of them with long, screened windows, all of them wallpapered and carpeted. In the corner of one room she'd installed a refrigerator and a two-burner electric range; in another there was a shower stall and a chemical toilet, and in the third there was a dresser and a bed. I slept on a pallet in the kitchen.

A few months after the accident, my father was allowed to go home. He was still in the body cast for the broken back. He lay in his BarcaLounger, nearly straight out. He'd been selling BarcaLoungers before the accident, and he always believed fervidly in the products he represented. Later on, when he went back to selling, he would treat the BarcaLounger mystically, saying, "This li'l honey saved my life," and he could make his voice quaver like a southern politician on Confederate Memorial Day. He wasn't even American. What he meant to say was that even a man crippled by pain and rendered immobile could master his convalescence, could still feel he had something useful to do with himself by going up and down in his BarcaLounger. In 1946, it was a whirlpool bath and physiotherapist in one molded slab of aluminum. He needed that little mechanism. He couldn't read, and this was before television, and the only radio station, from Ocala, was hard to get and even harder to understand. He and my mother I don't ever remember talking.

They had no money, of course. And then they exhausted the resources of eventual recovery — the donations of friends up north, my mother's relations in Canada, her bonds provided by a provident father.

So we left the three rooms. Things got sold that I'd never even seen unpacked. My mother's family was well-to-do, and my mother was a woman of taste. She'd been a decorator, and she'd accumulated things in Europe and in England and then in Montreal, where she'd met my father. Those things — Meissen things, Dresden things, Prague things, sketches she'd done in German and British museums, water-colour renderings she'd done for clients in Montreal, heavy silverware in a rich, burgundy velvet-lined case, candlesticks, cut-glass bowls, little framed paintings and etchings and cameos done on procelain or ivory — they meant nothing at all to me. She unwrapped them and cried; she tried to tell me the stories of their acquisition, the smuggling out. They meant nothing at all, to my shame. A BarcaLounger now — that was a valuable thing. When all my mother's boxes were empty, I carried them to the trash. All that I liked, and saved for a while, were the yellowed sheets of newspaper she'd packed them in, a dozen years before. I liked foreign-looking things. Some of the newspapers were in Gothic face. Some of them were in French.

So "a coloured man" was paid a dollar or two to move us from the three rooms into something we could afford. For the move someone donated a wheelchair, and so we walked across town — my mother, the coloured man and me, each carrying suitcases and boxes — and my father trailed behind, pushed indifferently by another part of the coloured man's family, called a coloured boy. He nudged my father down the main street (there were no sidewalks) with bursts of energy the way a boy might kick a stone for a few blocks until it careens under a car or somewhere out of reach. The first time my father's chair began to tip, causing him to wrench his back in an insane balancing act, the boy was canned, and I was appointed to finish the task. He made room on his lap for a suitcase and a lamp. His legs were pink, withered and scaly and would remain that way for years, until the rest of him started to shrink.

The new place was actually larger than the three rooms. It might have been called a house — it was detached but set back from the street, as a garage or a laundry house might have been. It gave us an address with an "A" at the end — something new in all our travels, "a sign" my mother said. Its virtue was that it was very, very cheap. The figure of ten dollars a month sticks in my mind. The facilities were outdoors, in an overgrown garden heavy with many other scents. Florida to me is always a collection of odours; it's the only thing I miss, and it's the first thing I notice about any new place I'm set down in. The outdoor commode — as my mother termed it — hadn't been used in a very long time; it was, like our small house, tilting and in need of paint. The virtue of an unused toilet cannot be exaggerated. It was quiet, neutral, and hygienic as nature itself. We soon took care of that, but rankness and a need for lime didn't set in for a few weeks. I don't know how my father used it, or even if he did; I suspect now my mother had arranged something with boards and a bucket and newspaper-linings in the house that she slopped outside every morning.

School was going on. I hadn't missed a day. I had started kindergarten outside of Atlanta and had put in a chunk of first grade in Gadsden, Alabama, and we had come to Leesburg, Florida, at the end of the first grade, before my father's accident, so that I was remembered by a few kids when second grade started. I usually didn't have that advantage. Most of the moves in our life were timed for summer, so that each September I began a new school. In Leesburg, Florida, in 1946, I had a small history.

I was more sociable in the days before my father's accident and the move across town. I remember, in those warm twilight evenings under the bare bulb of streetlights, the endless circling of bicycles in the fine dust of our lane; the week-end work-up games of baseball. I remember the first time I caught a pass thrown by an older boy and the buoyant worn pigskin, the fine black bubble of inner tube bursting between the laces. I had a curious side-arm throwing motion with a baseball that older boys watched and tried to imitate, without my control. Let's just say it was a southern town in post-war America, and so far as I knew anything about myself, I fitted in. I was accepted. Kick-the-can, fishing with doughballs, endless summers of bicycling, football and baseball; a subtropical life led out of doors, with rings of dust tamped down by sweat, scabs on the knees and elbows still forming or just falling off, a dingy, uneven tan, dingy, uneven blondness in all hair.

Things of course were working.

I was sociable. In the first grade, and in the summer, kids had come home with me; I went home with them. My mother baked, served, poured. Her exaggerated notion of Florida heat led her to elaborate formations of Jello and gallons of iced tea and lemonade and — universally rejected by everyone but me — buttermilk. She disapproved of Coke, that southern elixir, and wouldn't stock it. No one seemed to notice those three strange, papered rooms in the widow's house, or that my father was never home, or that my mother had an accent no one understood. She had no friends. My parents went nowhere, even on the five or six days a month when my father was home. He lived entirely for himself. My mother lived entirely for me. I found this a satisfactory arrangement. I lived entirely for the release from school.

After our move, Grady was my only friend. I remember walking over to his house after school. It was a small town in those days, and a child revealed everything about himself from the direction he nosed his bicycle in from the stands outside of school. Each cardinal compass point indicated who and what you were, what your father did and what your prospects in life were going to be. I was an exception because our little laundry shed of a house was the last white-occupied structure on that side of town. The county, I learned many years later, was 70 percent black. All street services — pavement, lights, water, sewage — ended half a block from our address, although houses like ours, unpainted and tilting on stilts, with old cars and refrigerators in the ungrassed yards, teeming with children and with sullen young men and women and old black women in straw hats with flowers on the brims, continued for many undemarcated blocks. My mother would embarrass me horribly by walking into Niggertown and running her hands over the heads of little girls and then standing in the yards calling up to women of her age, "I'm your new neighbour. We live just on the other side of the streetlight there. I hope you'll come over for tea some afternoon."

As I say, I was an exception, going east from school, down the Dixie Highway, and cutting through the alleys behind the stores where the Jim Crow serving windows were. Grady Stanridge went the other way, where the better families lived. They were the new people in town, people with businesses, people like us only younger and not from so far away. It's hard to understand, even now, that the parents were just starting out in life — they were in their twenties, the men navy and army veterans with tattoos and a hunger to repossess their lives; and that there were also a number of kids in my class who had never seen (and would never see) their fathers; and that the remarriage of young widows and subsequent moving to larger towns was a favourite topic in our first and second grades.

Grady and I strolled down the Dixie Highway. His father had the Western Auto store. Grady could take anything he wanted from the store — games, baseball gloves, fishing equipment. He was generous and I was greedy. I took a yo-yo — one of those deluxe Duncans at thirty-five cents — and a wooden vial of fish-hooks. Grady also took a yo-yo, and we were back on the shaded sidewalk, "walkin' our babies" and "loopin' the loop," when I saw my mother across the street, making her way from the cool, deep shade of the west side of town.

I prayed she wouldn't cross over. She had the Canadian custom of smothering me with "dears" and "darlings" and even "preciouses" in every conversation, and she even extended the custom to my little friends, as she called them. The one acceptable term of endearment — honey — she never used.

She was carrying a small package from the butcher's, and from the colour of stain on the outside I knew it to be liver, her — and my — favourite. We got it for ten cents a pound, since it wasn't considered fit for white consumption. It was assumed, whenever I was sent out to buy it, that we were getting it for our cleaning lady. I tried to keep my mother from going for it, since I knew she wouldn't go along with my lie.

She didn't see me. By the time we got to Grady's house I had mastered "cat in the cradle" and my middle finger was cold and white and nearly asphyxiated.

His house was Florida Moorish, with a tile roof, Mexican grillwork and rows of tall, narrow windows, curved on top. The outside was stucco; the grounds were well-tended, with oranges in the back, hibiscus and bougainvillaea along the trellises and a tightly tufted, low-pile lawn. The walkway was crushed limestone, rendered white in the Florida sun.

Mrs Stanridge was smoking in the living room, taking her afternoon break, it seemed, with a tall drink in a frosted, narrow glass. The house was very neat; even with all the windows — which were clean — the glass tables and the various ledges showed no dust. There was a large portrait hung over a small fireplace; the woman was stout and grey-haired. Her black dress and the rows of pearls and the wavy hair reminded me of a movie matron, the kind of stuffy lady Groucho Marx would spill something on.

Grady led me to the kitchen for iced tea, made in the southern fashion with no lemon and lots of sugar. Our house always featured lemons, and raw, tart foods were prized over all others. I used to chew rhubarb like celery, pop cranberries like cherries, suck lemons and chew limes. I didn't mind the way southerners cooked their food, with pots of vegetables boiling all day till they were soggy brown messes, but I realized my friends couldn't eat at my place at all because they found everything, from meat to vegetables to dessert, raw. Of course, with my father laid out in his BarcaLounger, and with my living on the edge of Niggertown, I understood I couldn't bring anyone home at all.

We heard Mrs Stanridge out in the living-room suddenly cursing and then shouting, "Grady, get in here!" She seemed to be frantic; all the order that had been apparent a few minutes earlier had been overturned. She'd opened the breakfront drawers and had silverware out on the dining table. She had stacks of newspapers scattered on the rug.

"Where is it?" she demanded. "Have you hidden it?"

"Hidden what, ma'am?"

"Hidden my purple flower pot. I have people coming over, and I went out to cut some flowers, and now I don't have my flower pot to put them in!"

"I don't even remember no purple flower pot!"

"It was purple. It was antique. It was right on the ledge under Big Mama's picture."

Grady looked at the ledge. Not even a dust ring; the ledge thinly underscored the painting, nothing else.

"It's the onliest thing I care about. I had that flower pot before I even met Mr Stanridge." Mrs Stanridge was almost whining.

"Well, don't look at me — I just got here," said Grady.

"I'm upset."

"I'll look for it."

"I think I know what happened."

"Maybe you took it to the kitchen."

"I should have put two and two together," she said. "It was that lady done it."

"What lady?"

"The cleaning lady."

"May-Lou?"

"You know May-Lou quit on me. The cleaning lady that answered the ad."

"Why would she want an old flower pot?"

"I seen her lifting it, even."

I could see a purple flower pot nestled nicely in the upper shelf of the breakfront. "Excuse me, ma'am," I said.

Grady was in the kitchen. He shouted out, "It ain't back here."

"She stole it, that's what. May-Lou might have broke it and not told me. But this one was too careful. She stole it."

"Ma'am?" I asked again.

"And her acting so superior. Like she was too good to clean a white lady's house. I even let her eat on my good plates."

"Is that it, there?" I pointed, and Grady's mother

reluctantly followed its direction. She hugged the pot like a rescued child, then set it back on the ledge and stepped away from it, just to admire it all over again.

"Thank God," she said. "And I promise you," she said, as though she were speaking directly to the pot or maybe someone's ashes inside it and not to Grady and me, who were walking our yo-yos just above carpet level, "I promise I ain't never hiring a white woman to do coloured work again!"

How easy it is for a boy, and then a young man, to write praises to his father. He sat there through my childhood and through my high-school years, and then he left, married two more times, and died. Never did we talk, never did he explain to me the passions (here I am again, calling them *passions* when I know for sure they were nothing but blind lusts) that drove him. And I have so deliberately mythologized him, the manly force in my life, the dark, romantic, French, medieval, libidinous force in my life, the foreign element in my life, believing somehow that his eighteen siblings, his six wives, his boxing career, his violence and his drinking and his police record, his infidelities, in some way ennoble *me*, tell me I'm not just the timid academic son of my mother's rectitude.

And she, who cleaned other people's houses while I attended school and my father reclined on his BarcaLounger, and finally returned to schoolteaching herself in Winnipeg after she finally left him, and who now lives alone in an apartment in Winnipeg, forgetting if she's eaten, forgetting to cook the things she's bought and keeps shoving into the refrigerator (the final smell in my catalogue of odours is the aroma of age, the rotting in the cold of orange-juice cans and Chinese dinners) — how easy it is for a boy and for a young man and even for a man now embarked on middle age to see his mother as nothing exceptional in the universe, nothing at all, an embarrassment in fact, against the extravagance of his father.

Mother, why couldn't we love you enough?

Identity

Identity

Porter, Reg and Hennie. My parents for several years. Mysteries to me, to each other. Gone now, even in name.

My earliest memory is of falling off an armchair when I was three and breaking my arm. A bad break, poorly mended. Even now the extended arm, with the elbow resting, barely grazes the tabletop. For the wrist and hand to conspire with gravity is an act of will. Think of the forearm as I do, a slow hypotenuse connecting that original fracture to a slightly skewered grand disclosure. Needless to say, I'm still waiting for it.

I'd been watching my father reading and writing in a Queen Anne chair. For years that memory stood as evidence that we'd been a normal, happy family. Father reading, son at his side, a little spill, nothing too serious. Despite the small imperfection it left me, it is a pleasant memory. It occurred to me since, however, that we never owned Queen Anne furniture, especially not in 1943, and that I cannot remember my father ever reading or writing. When I was thirteen and having to learn to read and write all over again, I discovered something else I'd always suspected: my father couldn't read or write at all.

That same year, 1943, I remember sitting on my tricycle at the top of a steep hill. This part of the memory is a moment, even now, of rather intense pleasure. And then I flung my legs out straight and rode like the breeze to the bottom of the little hill. Unfortunately, the hill was our driveway and the bottom of it was our garage door, and the door was down. From that episode, I received a bent nose, a broken collarbone and a skull fracture. After the fracture I became an epileptic. It was bad as a child, not so severe now. From internal evidence, you will conclude that I'm writing this as a man or forty-three.

Such are the sheltering memories of childhood. Or the preferred fictions of adulthood. I once overheard my mother, talking to a friend long after after I'd grown up, relate a more intriguing version of those same injuries. There'd never been a chair or a tricycle and garage door. There'd only been New Year's Eve, 1943, and a scrounged-up baby-sitter recommended by someone down at Sears, where my father worked. And she had a soldier husband who'd wangled a holiday pass, only to find her apartment empty. He saw our address on a piece of paper. He confronted her there, in our second-floor apartment on Reading Road, stabbed her and shot her visiting boyfriend, and then went to work on me, his only witness. So I was killed, at least to his satisfaction. I have never, consciously, been able to replay a single frame of that incident. So much for the theories of Freud or the plots of Ross Macdonald. I think of the armchair and the tricycle constantly.

Let more bones break, more moves be made. Those early memories are from Cincinnati — a freak appearance in our lives, a town that did not claim us — from deep in America, a country, as it turned out, that did not claim me either.

Turned out, not in the passive sense of a plot that runs its course, but in the active sense of total reversal, like a pocket being turned out, like deadbeats being turned out of a bar. There are millions like me on this continent (I know, I meet them everywhere) who constitute no bloc, and who, for all their numbers, have no champion. The implications radiate like angles from a protractor, like tracks from a roundhouse, though I'm unable to pursue them all. Think rather of Reg and Hennie Porter and me, lying just a degree or two off plumb, or the prime horizontal axis. Think of life, led slightly off balance.

In Pittsburgh in 1952 I was standing on the roof of an apartment building, with matches, a knife and rabbit-ears and sixty feet of antenna-feed. Double copper strand under opaque plastic. With matches I burned off an inch or so, stripped it with the knife, then spliced the copper onto the frail set of rabbit-ears that had come with our first television set. Then I lashed the whole contraption to the giant brick apartment-house chimney and crawled to the edge of the roof and called down, "How about it now?"

Staring down six floors to our opened window on the second floor was the closest thing I knew to an epileptic aura. The sidewalk yo-yo'd, close enough to step out on.

Peter Humphries, my only friend, was in our apartment. He was from the third floor. My parents both worked, so did his mother. His father did not seem to exist, even in memory.

He shouted up, "It's just a test pattern!"

He couldn't know that that was the whole point. I'd succeeded. It meant to me — though it was only Channel Nine in Steubenville, Ohio, or Seven in Wheeling, West Virginia — that features were materializing from outer space. New test patterns, new readers of local news, new advertisers, new street names, different phrasing of the same Tri-State weather, different politics: the mark of sophistication was access to all the channels. I'd exhausted KDKA, and the only NBC outlet before we got our own WIIC on Channel Eleven was Channel Six in Johnstown. Farther out in the mountains there was rumoured to be a Channel Ten in Altoona and a Channel Three downriver in Huntington, West Verginia. Pittsburgh, in other words, was an exciting place, if you had the right connections. Pittsburgh eventually got more than enough channels, but not in 1952. We were always deprived, last in everything, at least in the years I lived there. But with ingenuity and agility and rabbit-ears lashed to a chimney, hope existed for more than snow on channels two, three, six, seven, nine and thirteen, which was educational. On exceptional nights with my antenna pointing in the right direction I'd gotten Cleveland, and Chambersburg, almost in Maryland. A collector with luck could get a picture, however furry, and enough voice to make a positive identification, on every VHF channel, and he could pull in signals from four states, not counting freaks, which once, with the help of clouds, sunspots and a low-flying airplane, brought in Detroit and Buffalo.

The point is, I was king of the airwaves. I might not have known much about my parents or myself, or about Peter Humphries for that matter, but those questions never arose. I knew the important things, like call letters and the names of news readers and where to shop for Mercurys and Fords in Steubenville. It was the essence of my new-found teenagerliness to know everything about strangers and occult signals materializing from snow, and to know nothing at all about the forces that had made me, the scars and handicaps that were about to reclaim me.

All of this happened nearly thirty years ago. I haven't seen Pittsburgh in a quarter of a century, and probably all those familiar faces have scattered or died, although I still catch KDKA on the car radio, deep in the night. The magic is gone, but I'll stick with it till it fades completely to hear again those little neighbouring town names: Belle Vernon, Castle Shannon, Blawnox, Sewickley — names that were ushering in life to me, holding promises of jobs and adventure. Those were all threshold names, places I couldn't have located on an Allegheny County map, but that nevertheless were part of my private empire, my homeland, the back of my hand, whose borders were marked by the snowy extremities of Wheeling, Altoona, Chambersburg and Cleveland.

Peter Humphries is about to leave this story, but not before he leaves his mark, freshly, on me again. His mother was divorced — *divorcée* was one of those words, probably the only one, that a 1952 Pittsburgh kid pronounced in a self-consciously French way, to imbue it with its full freight of accompanying *negligées* and *lingerie* and *brassières* and of other things that came off in the night and suggested a rich inner life — she had dates, and Peter often slept over with us on nights when she planned to stay away. Or didn't plan, but stayed away anyway. As a cocktail waitress, then hostess, she didn't come home till three or four in the morning anyway, then slept till noon.

He might have been the gateway to my adolescence, but as it turned out — that phrase again — he was merely the last of my childhood friends. In a life of sharp and inexplicable and unmendable breaks, I have a special feeling for those friends of a special time and place. They seem to me, all of them, including my parents, prisoners of peculiar moments, waving at me from ice floes as dark waters widen between us. I remember all of them sharply, for they never were given a chance to grow out and modify; they were forever the last way I saw them, just as Pittsburgh is, which is to say they are essences of themselves and of my own poor perception of them. Even so, they give a surer sense of my own continuity than anything I can conjure in myself.

Peter was predictably avid for sex. He was riveted on the female body, every part of it, in ways that only a deeply troubled boy can be: hating it, fearing it, desiring it. He found my ignorance of it and my indifference to learning about it from him something of an affront. It marked me as being just a kid, which I was.

Being with Peter, the only friend I had, was like standing at the tip of an enormous funnel; all the sexual knowledge available to pubescent, provincial Americans in 1952 was swirling past me, and not a precious drop was wasted, not with Peter and his mother nearby. I wasn't in their apartment that often — they had the cheaper, one-bedroom model — but every time I entered it I was struck by the fumes of something lurid. Peter's mother wasn't much older than thirty, her hair was black and ringleted, her body lean and firm, her habits and language loose and leering. She'd strung clotheslines across the living-room, and her entire stock of lingerie and negligees was usually on display. Her job demanded a lot of buttressing and tressing, as well as display and ornamentation. The apartment was always dark, always a den, in deference to her strange professional hours. I'd never seen so many bottles and lotions; things to drink, to spray, to paint, to rub in, to rub off; it shocked me, the absence of normal food, the exclusion of anything not related to her body, skin and hair. The sofa was draped in suggestive dresses still in dry-cleaner's plastic, and the kitchen had hoisery soaking in the sink and a slab of meat defrosting on the counter. Peter slept in the dining room, on a foldaway cot that he had to dispose of in a closet every morning. They had a large television set, a "deal" she'd gotten from a motel close-out, but it didn't work.

What I responded to, of course, was the implicit savagery of that mother-son situation. She had nothing of the mother in her. She was a cruel woman who got by on lies about her youth, supported by candlelight and booze. A thirteen-year-old at home — who, as luck would have it, looked much older, with a jockey-like ropy body and tight, lined face of a child who wouldn't be growing much taller or broader — was the last thing in the world she would acknowledge as her own. They treated each other like husband and wife; he drank with her, gave her massages and sometimes crawled into bed with her.

There wasn't a time I visited when his mother was up and moving that I didn't come out of that apartment with something shocking to me, some hunk of flesh observed or knowledge that would stimulate me like some laboratory rat in an uncontrolled experiment. She would excite a centre of consciousness, but leave me without completion or comprehension. A moment caught in the kitchen, with Mrs Humphries talking casually of "ragging it" and needing some peace and quiet; of a man's voice muffled by the door to her bedroom shouting out, "Hey, what the —?"

The most frightening moment didn't concern her at all. It was with Peter alone. "Hey, want to see something? Look in here." And before I could stop him, he was into his mother's clothes, underwear first, then the dresses and finally the make-up, all very professionally applied. We avoided each other for a few weeks after that. He'd let something drop.

My mother called her "The Slut." — Peter called her "her" and "she." To have been the son of such a woman, to have absorbed the full blast without any shield (even grown men could take her only one night at a time) was a formula for disaster more potent than even my own. I envied him the nakedness of things in his life. His mother was to me, thanks to the luxury of deflection, like a pair of 3-D glasses on the world; things I couldn't have noticed in my mother or in my secretive parents stood in sharp relief thanks to her. And thanks to Peter, on those nights he'd shared my bed, I learned how women were built, what Kotexes were for, where "it" went and how it got there. Thanks to Peter, I became a statistically normal American pre-teen, as judged by the Kinsey Foundation.

In most areas of development, I was keeping pace. Peter was the sexual guide, his mother the sexual quarry and my parents, the ultimately mysterious Reg and Hennie, were receding nicely from me as peers took over. A career based on my odd little passion for resolving distant images, for pulling in signals, was suggesting itself. It would be consistent with all this data to say that I grew up to become an astronomer, monitoring some deep-dish radio telescope on a thin-aired mountaintop far from the murk of Pittsburgh. But even as children we are not miniatures of an eventual self. Perhaps we are scouts; more daring and treacherous than the troops we lead, than the adults we become.

I have spoken of all the things I knew in 1952. What I didn't know was about to kill me. I died in 1952, not from my epilepsy or a fall from a sixth floor or an electric jolt or anything else from that world of Pittsburgh or Peter Humphries. These fragments stand out to me now, against a black background, and that seems to be the nature of childhood as it bleeds into adolescence: that we see faces without the lies and sympathies of self-protection, we can live events without antecedent or consequence. They appear tantalizingly sharp, but in a veil of snow and static: we can make them out, but then they fade and are no more.

My parents: Reg and Hennie Porter. My name is Philip. Phil Porter. Reg was working in a department store called Rosenbaum's in downtown Pittsburgh. It's been gone a quarter of a century now, so I'll not disguise any of these names. Names are treacherous anyway.

Reg was a good-looking man, about fifty, with dense, white chest hair and forearms thick as Popeye's, hairy and tattooed *"Amor Vincit"* in a thin, unfurled banner under a starlet's face, neck and bare shoulders down to what promised to be indecent cleavage. He'd been married twice before, so far as I knew, and I'd found that out only when I overheard it. It didn't seem safe to ask if he had other children, though they'd hardly be kids. He might have married at twenty or less, so conceivably there were other Porters around, somewhere in New England, where he came from. He usually had the accent to prove it. But those kids could be thirty. My parents had been married eighteen years — I knew that from their number of anniversaries. I loved every aspect of that man.

If I could stop time, or stop narration, I would linger on the lean, graceful, grey-haired buxom figure of my mother (as she suddenly stands out to me) in the late summer of 1952. She was a woman softened by the grey in her hair, made younger by it (I don't remember her dark-haired, but I suspect she had looked almost masculine, the kind of young woman who must have a very handsome brother somewhere; a face that seems to find its resolution in the opposite sex). She hadn't married till thirty-two. Grey hair had finally focused her face, the way a beard might define an otherwise unspectacular set of features.

I've said enough. You will know already that the story is beginning to turn inside out. I had Oedipal longings — still do, doubtless, since I've never consciously considered them or worked them out — and my hours of staring into snowy screens, rejoicing with any faint signal, offers to me now a portrait of sublimation. There is sexual energy sparking over the gaps. And all my attempts at refining the images are doomed because the interference is built in: in my brain where blood vessels and nerve endings just don't quite reach, where some blunt or sharp object — in my case, a shard of bone — sliced through. And of the other connections to family and to place and even to language, I cannot speak at all. Those were things out on the street, outside of me entirely, about to knock on our door.

All right. People wonder what it's like to die, and since I've done it several hundred little-bad times and a few great convulsive big-bad times, and have died in other ways, too, I'll start small and build.

Dying is like this. You are twelve, coming back to the apartment after school. Picture it September, those scratchy days when the heat is up and school's not serious yet and the summer pursuits are still operative. I came home with a cherry sno-cone, about four o'clock. The front door was half open. Inside were half-packed boxes, all over the place, where selections of our things had been thrown in. My mother dashed from the kitchen to another opened box, a stack of china against her bosom, and eased them into the box and scrunched some pages of the *Post-Gazette* around them. She was a careful packer, and this was not careful packing. And because of my unexpected entrance, my shocked silence, her concentration, she did not see me. I caught her in expressions I'd never seen before; she was smaller, younger, sexier than she'd ever appeared before, all the more so for her obvious distress, or distraction, or anger — whatever indefinable thing it was. We'd moved many times before, and usually under bad conditions — to towns we didn't know and where we had no address. Those moves were chance things: pack up the car, flee a city and travel to a place where a job might be waiting. Then find an apartment after a few days in a squalid hotel, unpack, put the boy in school. We'd sometimes moved when rent was due; my father was so calm about it he could meet a landlord at the door, listen politely to his demand, reach in his pocket for the chequebook, saying all the time, "Sure, sure," and then slap his forehead, "God, forgot it!"

"That's okay, what about tomorrow?" the landlord would say.

"Right you are," my father would say, "first thing in

the morning." And two hours later we'd be at the outskirts of town, heading deeper into America.

My death was standing at the open door of my apartment, seeing my mother run from the kitchen clutching a stack of plates against her blouse and dropping them into a box, and thinking:

1. We're moving.
2. We're skipping.
3. Something terrible is happening.
4. Christ, my mother is a *sexy* woman.
   a) On reflection, this last insight is tempered by the further insight that nearly any woman, when viewed unannounced, in the privacy of her living-room, is sexy. That is, the act of observing is sexy.
   b) She legitimately was sexy. Her hair was up, but falling down, the grey and the black, and she was in slacks and one of my father's shirts, and she was looking good.
   c) Sexiness, if I am now to lift it from any immediate context or application to any particular woman, is (for me) an appearance that borders on slovenliness. Sex will never embrace me in tennis shorts, in a bikini, or in any fetishistic combination of high heels and low neckline. Sex is the look that says, "Help me out of these clothes," or shows that things she's wearing are a constriction, not an attraction.

On that late summer day in 1952, standing quietly and excitedly in the door of our apartment that was soon not to be our apartment, I had a seizure. When I woke up a few minutes later, my mother was holding the wooden spoon she used to keep me from biting my own tongue (what abuse that spoon had taken, over the years!). My mind was absolutely clean: I woke up remembering only that I knew something about my mother. And I knew something else: that this move was different from the others. In this one, the furniture was staying, but papers I'd never seen before were littering the floor. Papers in old leather folders with the crushed ribbons of official documents that had not been untied in a generation. When I could walk, she helped me back to the bedroom. She indicated that I should fall over my parents' double bed, but I ritually opened my own bedroom door.

Sitting on my bed was my father. I saw him in bright colour, the way only an epileptic can see the world, after an attack. I saw every pore, every hair, intensely sharp. I would not have recognized him on the street. He was crying, and it looked to me that he had been crying for hours and that he had nothing left to cry with. His shirt buttons were torn open, but his tie was still knotted, red silk over chest hair. His sleeves were rolled back, those massive arms lay helpless at his side and the cuff-links were still stuck in the cuffs, and I worried that they'd fall out. My mother pushed me hard, out of my room and into theirs, and I was still groggy two hours later when she put two suitcases in my hands and told me to march quickly and quietly to the car, which was parked in the alley.

We headed north towards Buffalo and slipped through the middle of New York state all night long. He knew where he was going, though he didn't tell me. Around two o'clock in the morning he pulled into a large motel between Syracuse and Utica, waking me again, almost shaking me to make sure I was awake.

"Philip," he said, all the time shaking me. "Philip, until I tell you it's okay to talk, I don't want you to say a word. Not one word. Not even if someone talks to you, understand?"

"Even if things seem wrong," my mother said. "Even if you don't understand a thing."

At three in the morning my father and I went prowling through the parking lot of that large motel while my mother slept in the car. I was scouting for a licence plate and a dollar bounty offered by my father. Finally I found one, on a black, pre-war Ford. My father stripped it of its plate — like Pennsylvania, they had only a rear plate — and put it on our car. Our plate was creased until it snapped, then buried. At five o'clock we were on the road again, over the Adirondacks, with my mother driving. They were talking now of "the border," and the motels were flying two sets of flags, the American and a red British one, and ads were appearing for duty-free items. When the customs houses were in view, she pulled off to the side. My father took over. "Tell him," he told my mother and she turned around to face me.

"In a minute we'll be going into Canada. Canada is where your father and I come from." She flashed some of those documents in front of me. "We're going to Montreal. We have relatives in Montreal."

I still had not spoken, could not speak.

"Our name will change when we go over the border. Forget all you ever know about Porter. Our real name is Carry-A. Like this — see?" She showed me a plastic-coated green-framed card with an old picture of my father on it. I couldn't pronounce the name, but the letters bit into my brain. Réjean Carrier.

"What's my name?" I asked.

"I thought I told you to shut up," said my father.

There were two cars in front of us. My father found a radio station playing strange music in a foreign language.

"You can be anything you want to be," said my mother.

North

North

In the beginning, my mother would meet me at the "*Garçons*" side of Papineau School. She might have been the tallest woman in the east end of Montreal in the early fifties. I was walking with my friend Mick. I was thirteen, and he was older but smaller. From the neck up he looked twenty. He was in my cousin Dollard's class. He had discovered me on the first day of school, standing by the iron gate looking puzzled. "Take the garkons," he had advised, under his breath. *Garkons* was an early word in my private vocabulary. In the beginning, I had to trust strangers' pronunciations, or worse, my own.

"You're not one of them, are you, eh?" I liked that; *them* — it sounded science-fictiony. How could he tell? Getting no answer, he went on, "My old lady, she ups and marries this Frog. What's your story?"

My story? Same old story, too preposterous. Until the week before, I'd been Phil Porter, content but lonely, riding the airwaves of Pittsburgh, attaching rabbit-ears to our apartmenthouse chimney, pulling in seven channels from adjacent states. All I said to Mick that first day was, "My name's Carrier, but I'm not French."

"Me too. Bloody Fortin. All the Fortins in my family are English and all the Sweeneys are French. Funny, eh? Where you from — the States? Vermont?"

Pittsburgh rang no bells for Mick Fortin. He only knew the cities that sent us tourists — Burlington, Plattsburgh, and half of Harlem, plus the cozy loop of the old NHL. "Do you have a job yet?" he asked me, and I feared for a minute that a job was required in this new world of the French eighth grade, like my pens and tie and white shirt for school. Mick was too ignorant, too solicitous, too eager with his confessions to be trusted. He promised me a job in the spring, down along St Catherine Street, passing out peep-show leaflets to the Yanks. "You've heard of Lili St Cyr, eh?" I hadn't, but nodded. "All you gotta do is say, 'C'mon'n see her! Lili St Cyr's younger and sexier sister!' All the girls down there call themselves St Cyr something, Mimi or Fifi. The Yanks, they eat it up." In the beginning, I welcomed my mother's intervention.

We'd left Pittsburgh in the middle of the night. My father had assaulted a man at work. He'd found him seated at his desk, feet on an opened drawer, packing up my father's pictures and souvenirs. A younger man, brought in from the outside. He got his first three words in — "You're out, Porter" — and then my father grabbed his ankles and spilled him backwards out of the chair. Then he picked him off the floor and shoved him only once, and the new manager found himself bursting through fresh dry-wall and skidding to a halt by the water cooler. And

my father caught the first elevator to Canada, convinced
that no one knew his secret name and true identity. Some
time in the middle of that night, somewhere in the middle
of upstate New York, my father Reg Porter reverted to
Réjean Carrier, and I was allowed to retain my name of
Phil, but Porter was taken from me forever. "You
weren't born in Cincinnati like we always said," my
mother explained. "I'm sorry, but we had to tell you that.
You were born in Montreal."

We moved into the apartment of his older brother,
Théophile. I bumped Dollard from his room, and my
parents took the living-room sofa. Théophile's six
daughters were married, or in the Church. In a pantry-
sized bedroom off the kitchen lived Aunt Louise who'd
married an American in Woonsocket and seen all three of
her sons go down with the *Dorchester* in 1942. She didn't
speak, she only lit candles, and the smell of wax
permeated the apartment. My mother would have the
sheets and pillows stored away each morning by seven
o'clock, and I don't think they went out during the day. I
don't know what they and my aunt Béatrice, who spoke
no English, did all day.

The first big fight had been over my schooling. School
had been in session nearly a month when we arrived on
Théophile's doorstep. I hadn't known a word of French,
though I began collecting words from Dollard that first
day. From him, everything began with "*maudit . . .* "
and ended with " *. . . de Christ sanglant.*" In a week I
knew some nouns and adjectives; no verbs, no sentences.
French neutralized my mother's education; she was like a
silent actress. I learned to read her eyes, her lips, and to
listen to her breathing, and her feelings came through like
captions. She would nod her head and say, "wee-wee,"

which made the simplest French words come out like baby-talk. She was one of those western Canadians of profound good will and solid background, educated and sophisticated and acutely alert to conditions in every part of the world, who could not utter a syllable of French without a painful contortion of head, neck, eyes and lips. She was convinced that the French language was a deliberate debauchery of logic, and that people who persisted in speaking it did so to cloak the particulars of a nefarious design, behind which could be detected the gnarled, bejewelled claws of the Papacy. She was, of course, too well-bred to breathe a word of this suspicion to anyone but me. All evening, then, as she stood next to Béatrice at the sink, peeling, washing, baking and frying our food, it was Béatrice's steady stream of incomprehensible opinions and my mother's head-jerking wee-wees, the smell of wax and Dollard's obscene mutterings that initiated me into a world that would be, for all I knew, mine forever.

My mother had wanted to send me to an English school, although the nearest one was at the end of two trolley rides. I was silent about it. English would obviously be easier, but not necessarily preferable. I wanted to belong, and no one I knew in Montreal spoke English, except my mother. Canadian schools, my mother said, were light-years ahead of American, and English was the only language for an intelligent boy who didn't want to become a priest. French school was so fundamentally *wrong*, it was alluring to contemplate. For the first time in my life no one could possibly expect anything from me. Théophile settled it. He was a member of the St-Jean-Baptiste Society. No one living under his roof would even study English, let alone go to school in it. Anyway, it wasn't safe. There was no way to get to an English school that didn't cut through the middle of the Jewish ghetto, where French boys were routinely butchered. He had this on good authority, though they didn't dare print it in the communist press. Dozens of French boys had disappeared — altar boys — they only used the purest blood. My mother retired to the bathroom. My father chimed in, "They'd kill him on this street, for sure. They'd kill any kid on this street if he went to an English school."

Tricks of the mind. Even in my memories of those three strange years, nuns and classmates seem to be speaking to me in English — a clear violation of the natural universe — and I seem to be writing papers and speaking up in class, always in English. This is clearly not so, for there's a band of three years in my life when I discovered nature where even now I'm still learning the English names. Fish, trees, flowers, weeds, foods, drinks can all send me to the dictionary. And the discovery of myself as a sexual creature — slightly different from the discovery of sex itself — that too is a function of French.

For the first time in my life I felt that school was a punishment. Nuns were wardens, the cracking of the cane was arbitrary and malicious. We were prisoners serving time for a crime whose nature would presently be revealed. I assumed my guilt; it was my ignorance of the charge, not my innocence, that made the confusion so painful.

I was caned in the second week. The impossible had happened *to me*. I was made to mumble an act of contrition. I wasn't even Catholic. "*Pourquoi ça?*" I kept demanding as the cane kept whizzing down, day after day for a week. Even harder, for my question suggested arrogance. There would be no explanation. He was a Brother of the Order of Mary, who otherwise smiled at me when he passed me in the halls. In the second week, Soeur Timothée let it out: my cousin Dollard had been cutting classes and acting unrepentant to the brothers. "*Hôtage!*" she hissed at me, taking over the caning. "*Tu sais hôtage?*" I learned quickly enough. Finally my mother noticed the backs of my hands, the welts and bruises. She raged, with only my father and me to understand her.

"Discipline!" he exclaimed. "That's what they give, and he has to learn to take it!" I hadn't told them about Dollard. I hadn't even told Dollard about the punishment I was taking on his behalf, but I hoped word would drift back to him before my fingers fell off. My father was defending them, in his way. Compared to *his* years with the brothers, when he'd been given to them at the age of five for eventual priesthood, my life had been one of silken pillows. If my hands hadn't been as soft as a girl's there wouldn't even be bruises. "Look at Dollard's hands — they're like hockey gloves," he shouted. My father wasn't defending the church — he hated it from the depths of his bowels — but he revered its implacable authority. Whatever they did to you, you should be grateful; it made you tough enough in later life to keep telling them to go to hell.

"Discipline!" my mother raged. "You fools. You bloody fools — is that what discipline is to you? Treating children like animals? Beating them into submission? It's medieval, it's madness. You're crazy, can't you see? You're twisted, and I won't have you twisting your son the same way." She grabbed my hands and clutched my fists to her chest. "Discipline isn't just learning how to take pain. Discipline doesn't mean you have to be stupid. God, if the bloody Church told you tomorrow the earth was flat, you'd start telling yourselves you knew it was flat all along, right? Wouldn't you? Wouldn't you?"

I felt guilty, terribly guilty, bringing on such an argument. There was injustice here, on every side. My father — that unemployed, wrecked shell of a man — was standing in for Théophile and Dollard, whose stupidities were unassailable, and for the brothers at school whose cruelties, given the system, were unremarkable and fairly even-handed. My father hadn't been inside a church in forty years, not since he'd fled the barbarities of a harsher time and place and taken those memories, that rage, into the streets of Montreal and beyond. But against my mother, his words and logic were pathetic.

Now his voice was weary. "Okay," he admitted. His fists were heavy in front of his face; he kept balling them up and flinging them open. "You don't know how they think. How they work . . . . It's . . . . " and he shrugged his shoulders, empty of words. I wanted to complete it for him; I understood more about it than he ever would. What the brothers were doing to me to get to Dollard would have worked in any family in Papineau School — we were the freaks. I was suffering a complicated shame. Then my father came up with a new inspiration. "You think the Sistine Chapel was painted without discipline?" There was a series of pictures taped to the dining-room wallpaper, cut from the pages of *Life* magazine, celebrating Vatican art. The Sistine Chapel won many arguments in the Hochelaga district of Montreal in the early fifties.

In memory, Pittsburgh came bursting through like a freak radio signal. In my junior-high classes, the sexes had mingled, the girls had steamed and giggled in a heavy-breasted, painted-up pool of pubescent sexuality. They wore whatever the could get away with. They stuffed lewd and graphic promises through the ventilation slats of our lockers and raced for the girls' rooms between classes to smoke like little hellions. They were utterly available, begging to be touched.

But in Papineau we entered and left by the "*Garçons*" and "*Filles*" sides of the building, as though joint entombment for eight hours a day was concession enough to sordid physiology; the nuns and brothers even positioned themselves like Holy Crossing Guards two and three blocks away, to prolong the segregation. Coeducation was a sad fact of life, but withering disapproval could safeguard our innocence at least till high school. The girls wore black jumpers and no make-up, and their hair was cut uniformly straight and short. Not a pony-tail, not a bleach job in the lot. I'd been too young in Pittsburgh to act on my impulses, to inhale those lusty vapours rising from the breeding pens of an American junior high school. Now, I felt, I could. Just turn me loose, anywhere in America. I burned in hell, remembering it.

And then, miraculously, the nuns gave me a girl. At four o'clock after another gruelling day of faint comprehension, Soeur Timothée told me to stay after class — not for discipline — but to meet my own, private, ninth-grade tutor, Thérèse Aulérie. Tutor and general *ange gardien* in everything from penmanship (we were on the continental system, with crossed sevens, ones like giant carat marks; whenever I require assurance that indeed these things happened to me I have it still, in my handwriting) to the foundations of all advanced knowledge: Latin, French and the Catholic religion. Thérèse was Papineau's outstanding student in Classics, French, Apologetics and even Natural Science.

Ninth-grade girls back in Pittsburgh simply had more going for them than Thérèse Aulérie, despite her brilliance. There was first of all the question of make-up, that bright impasto of sexual longing, so innovatively applied by American teenagers. They had Hollywood and television to guide them, not to mention the Terry Moore sweaters stretched over the mountain-building process we runty seventh and eighth graders could measure by the week, if not the hour (just as I scrutinized my chin for each new black whisker, cherished each new fissure in my cracking vocal chords and checked every inch of my body for other rampant endocrinal signposts worth flaunting).

In Papineau, everything was hidden. Girls in jumpers, no make-up, no hair-styles; they took their cues from Soeur Timothée. But Thérèse Aulérie was a slight improvement. She had the palest skin and the greenest eyes I had ever seen (it was the first time I'd been forced to focus on such adult, literary features as fine skin and expressive eyes), and lips that were natural and pink to a sheen of edibility. She wore clear nail polish — a vanity, she later confessed — and the only other exposed acreage of flesh, her cheeks, were delicately flushed, and dimpled. Her voice was low and throaty, a woman's voice coming from the face of Margaret O'Brien. She looked so *nearly* familiar it seemed impossible that she didn't speak a word of English and even regarded hearing it as a low-grade, unclassifiable sin.

We began with Apologetics. We had a small handbook of Nuns and Monks and Teaching Orders, and my first job was to learn how to identify the various orders by their special dress, their expertise, their place and date of founding. I'd thought of them as exotic wildlife anyway: tracking them with an imprimatured bestiary seemed a natural way of pinning them down. I started rattling off their dates and countries of origin with an ease that astonished her, leaving Thérèse to fill in the substantive issues — for her at least: were they known best for their piety or their charity? Their compassion or courage? Their humility or brilliance? Most of our brothers were Marists, with a Sacred Heart in the chapel. The nuns were mainly our local Greys and Ursulines, but a sharp eye could spot a Blessed Virgin on special assignment. This part was easy, like learning the makes and models of new cars. Thérèse, once she dropped the ninth-grade condescension, was full of unofficial data about every order. *Les laides, les bêtes, les gueules, les graisses*. Soeur Timothée, I learned, was called Soeur La Morse. "What's a *morse*?" I asked, and Thérèse tapped imaginary tusks and made deep seal-like grunts. "Walrus!" I laughed, and she repeated, in a voice suddenly high and girlish, "wal-russ." In fact, Thérèse Aulérie, for all her grades and piety and possible calling as a Sister of Charity, was a sharp little cookie who began confiding to me of her visits to the States, a Chinese restaurant she'd been taken to in Manchester, New Hampshire, the week-ends at Old Orchard Beach and the television she'd stared at for a solid, slothful week-end in a Burlington motel. She'd even gone to New York City when she was six, and she still had all the postcards. In her America, everyone spoke French except the people on television.

"Did you really go to school in America?" she asked in French. My French wasn't good enough to answer more than an authentic, Dollardish "*ouai*." No way to describe its wonders.

"*Comme Hartchie*?" she asked. "*Et Véronique?*"

It took me a few seconds to catch on. "*Et Juggie aussi*," I laughed.

"Ah, Juggie," she nodded gravely. "*Juggie j'aime beaucoup.*"

We sighed; I for the multiplicity of stories I couldn't build upon, the impossibility of representing myself in a language I didn't know, or to a girl who didn't know mine.

"*Et ton nom, était-il toujours Carrier là-bas?*"

It didn't seem strange to her that people changed names when they crossed the border. In America, I tried to explain, we'd sailed under a flag of translation. "*Porter*," she tried, in her curious, high-pitched English. "*Non, c'est laid, ce nom-là. Carrier, c'est un bon nom canadien.*"

I answered, with sad conviction sealing the linguistic gaps, "Anyway, names *ne fait rien.*"

She drew her desk closer. "*Épeles mon nom de famille. Divines.* Go ahead. Try!"

"A-U —" I began. And she giggled, shaking her head.

"*Mon* vrai *nom. Commences avec 'o,'* like dis, eh?" I loved it when she tried her English. It came out like Dollard's, but without the threat. "*C'est le vrai français, mon nom, de la France, pas d'ici.*" She wrote, "O'L —"

"O'Leery?" I spelled.

"O'Leary," she corrected. "*Ça c'est le nom de mon grand-père.*" She turned the paper as though admiring a work of art. "Nice," she said.

I felt I'd been handed a powerful interpretive tool, but I didn't yet know how to wield it. Here I was, a Carrier who spoke no French, and she was an O'Leary who read "Archie" comic books but knew no English, and we were together in a darkening classroom in Montreal under a cross, flanked by the photos of the Cardinal of Montreal and the Holy Father. We were linked beyond simple assignments. My guardian angel, according to Sister Walrus, who would lead me from ignorance to power, just as the sisters and brothers would lead me from hellfire to righteousness.

Thérèse closed her book after the quiz on habits and orders and asked me, slowly and with grand gestures, can girls (she pointed to herself) in the ninth grade in America really wear lipstick (she ran her pinkie over her lips) and dress they way they want? She formed a gentle, wavy outline with her hands, passing over an imaginary female form just outside her square-cut jumper with all the lewdness (I fantasized) of a sailor describing his last night's conquest. Can they really go out on dates? She clawed my wrist at the word "*rendez-vous.*" Those new words burned themselves in my brain: *maquillage . . . se habiller comme l'on veut . . . rendez-vous*. Do they all have cars? How late can they stay out? She was suddenly like a little girl, and somewhere in the late fall gloom, and then under the yellow globes of a four-thirty northern autumn night, I started imagining a Thérèse O'Leary in make-up, and I noticed how her jumper flared out modestly in front and filled out gently in the rear, and how a nice wide belt would have pinched it together, just right. And how her voice, that deep French purr, would have driven American boys wild.

It must have been in those weeks in our daily hour after school and in our walks away from school for two low, mean, icy, glorious unsupervised blocks to her trolley stop that the current in our little relationship shifted direction. By the end of our first month, her English improved to the level of fairly detailed conversation. I rummaged through my mother's suitcase and found a proper belt. Once on a Saturday I passed her with her parents at Dupuis Frères department store, and she was in a sweater and skirt, wearing lipstick and pearl earrings.

I came to think of my five hours a week with Thérèse as my parole from solitary. I came to understand my mother's use of the word "drab" to describe the interiors and the streets, the minds and souls and conversations of east-end Montreal. One big icy puddle of frozen gutter water, devoid of joy, colour, laughter, pleasure, intellect or art. School and home and church and the narrow east-end streets that connect them are the same colour even now in my memory, linked in a language that I didn't understand except through its rhythms. Recitations in class took on a dirge-like quality, like the repeated Hail Marys on Sunday radio. Eventually even I, who knew neither Latin nor French nor the lists of martyrs to the Iroquois, could stand and repeat the proper syllables. The name of our school, Papineau, figured in Quebec history as a great patriot who had tried to rid the province of English and American influences, and his name was repeated on the street outside and on panel trucks and signboards of plumbers and plasterers and in the *épicerie* where Aunt Béatrice did her shopping. It seemed slightly blasphemous, like Latin ballplayers carrying the name of Jesus. The same few names popped up everywhere, with six Tremblays in my class and over half of us clustered alphabetically at "La—" and nearly all of us ending in "—ier." Our names were as predictable as Armenians', as unmistakable as Chinese, and mine was one of the commonest. We were common, and we learned to feel comfortable only in the presence of other *bons noms canadiens*. "Ignorance!" my mother had cried one night, fleeing the dinner table. She had bought red table napkins, something to brighten the winter gloom, and my uncle had slammed his to the floor, saying it would "*causer l'acide.*"

And so, my mother began meeting me after school, a block from where I parted from Thérèse. Sometimes we would ride the trolley downtown and go into Eaton's or Ogilvy's — places that felt off-limits to the rest of the family. And there I would glow in the mystical power of speaking English, a power that wasn't furtive or dirty, as it felt in the apartment. The power of not having to scratch for words and not biting back the urge to comment, or even attack.

On the furniture floor of Eaton's she said, "I worked here, you know. I was even the head of this whole department." We walked through the model home, the half-dozen bedrooms and dining-rooms featuring different styles of decoration. "Your father was one of the salesmen. Until I saw him, I never even bothered learning their names. I knew he was wrong for me. Knew from the beginning." No one recognized her now, though it had been only thirteen years. She'd gone to the States, been lost to history. "I was a very different woman in those days. I want you to understand that. It wasn't easy, back then, in this city. Women couldn't even vote. And they don't accept women here, not English women, not Protestant women. They'll never do that." I could read her eyes and breath; I wanted to avoid the tears that I knew were coming. "I deserve it all, don't I? Sleeping on a floor in Hochelaga. No wonder they don't want to remember me — I must look a sight." She trailed her fingers in the dust of the dining-room tables and nightstands, then took me up to the cafeteria on the top floor. We would have our tea and scones, sometimes served with a little lemon curd. She perked up, over tea. "I don't want you to despise them. They are what they are. Deep down, they're good people. They've taken us in when we could have ended up . . . I don't want to think how we could have ended up, and they've shared what they have. But I *do* resent them, I can't help it. I resent their tight little ways, not with money — darling, do you understand what I'm saying? Their fist-like little souls, always ready to fight you or slink away like a beaten dog — does that make sense? I don't want you growing up like them."

It was always harder, going back to Hochelaga after scones and lemon curd and a few hours of uninterrupted English. The urge to speak our language seemed to die when the trolley crossed St Lawrence. In a few weeks I would reach a linguistic equilibrium, and I probably could have been happy enough — given endless lemon curd or access to Thérèse O'Leary — existing like a child in either world. But I was being forced, subtly at first, every day, to make moral decisions. French or English were the terms, but they were merely covers for personalities inside and out that I wanted to keep hidden.

One Friday in early December my mother held me back from school. Quietly, she motioned me to put on my coat. We took the trolley downtown not quite to Eaton's, then walked up to Sherbrooke past the clean grey limestone and green copper roofs of McGill University, that Gibraltar of Englishness. "Some day you'll go here," she said. "I don't care what it takes or if you graduate from French school or American schools — they'll have to let you in." I welcomed her authority. We stood on Milton Street just outside the iron railings; I wanted to reach inside. I could understand the shouts of the students, their quiet conversations as young couples passed us on the sidewalk.

"Who are those men in black robes?" I asked. "Judges?"

"Professors," she said. "This is the greatest university in the world." She so rarely allowed herself the luxury of an uncontested assertion — "too American" was her feeling about any claim to undisputed superiority — that I knew I'd been handed an indisputable fact. I trusted my mother more than any nun, even more than any Jesuit. "Come," she said, and we turned down Prince Arthur, through a maze of small half-streets that curled between Pine and St Urbain. We stopped in front of a tall apartment block of dull cherry brick, where long icicles hung over the door. "I want you to meet an important person in my life," she said. "And in yours, I hope."

"Who?" And I swear, had she asked me, *Who do you think*? I would have answered, *My father. My real father*. There was something monumental inside, the clarity behind all the confusions. Her gloved finger ran down the row of buzzers. At "Perleman, E." she stopped.

We were buzzed inside. My mother's hands were shaking. "Ella is a brilliant woman. A professor at McGill." In the tiny elevator she whispered, "I used to live right here, in this building. When I came back from England and got that job at Eaton's."

"With her?"

"I called her last week. I haven't seen her in thirteen years. She sounded —" and her voice was stumbling now, "grand. She's a grand girl."

"You used to get letters from her," I remembered. Back in Pittsburgh I saved the high-denomination Canadian stamps that came to us on those thick envelopes from Montreal.

"She's my dearest friend. The times we had! Oh, Lord, the times . . ."

Ella was standing by the elevator, a gnome-like woman of my mother's age, wrapped in a stiff green skirt and a man's sweater that smothered her body like a duffel bag. My mother had to stoop to hug her, and she was already losing control, while Ella merely patted her back and shoulders and murmured "There, there, Hennie," in what seemed to be a lilting accent. Her dark brown eyes were wide and sad, and her skin was a fine, translucent pink. Her hair was entirely grey and nearly as short as mine. She looked, I thought, like Albert Einstein. She pulled us down the hall to her opened apartment door. I could easily see over her head into a living-room dingy with smoke and oppressive with apartment heat. It must have been eighty-five degrees inside, and I started clawing desperately at my scarf and *tuque*, as she picked up a lavender shawl and draped it over her shoulders.

"Dolly," she called out, and a gaunt woman, slightly younger, shuffled out from the bedroom. "This is Henny, whom I've spoken so much about. And her boy, Philip." I nodded, regretting the day of school I was missing. "This is Dolly. Dolly works in the accounts office at McGill. So." Dolly took that as a sign to go to the kitchen and prepare some tea.

If McGill was the world's finest university and Ella one of its professors, I reasoned that she must be the smartest woman in the world. That went a long way to forgiving her appearance and her strange habits. She picked up a pipe from the nearest coffee table, and as she sucked on it, drawing in the flame, I could swear it *was* Einstein peering at me over the flame and bowl of the pipe. My mother was bearing up. She too was watching me, and I was behaving myself; nothing strange about a woman smoking a pipe. It was impossible to think of Ella ever crying, ever getting too personal and sentimental, and for that I was grateful.

"So. You must forgive two old women who haven't seen each other . . . " Ella and my mother were seated across from me on the sofa, and Ella was patting my mother's hand. "I must say you look well, Hennie, everything considered. Some of us got old rather quickly."

"You look just the same, Ella." My mother was staring down at her lap, at Ella's hand.

"Well, nothing ever happens in Montreal, so who can tell? The city hasn't changed one bit. The things we fought for have gradually come to pass — we can vote now, Hennie — isn't that grand? But the workers are still oppressed and the church still runs things and the police behave like Tartars and the corruption is still a public joke and our candidates still lose their deposits every election. Remember our election parties?" My mother smiled, and Ella let out a sharp bark of a laugh. "We'd all come back here to this apartment" — she was looking at me again — "the finest candidates who ever ran for public office in this country, and we'd sit around sipping sherry waiting for a call. And outside the police were waiting. If we'd actually won we'd have gone directly to jail. Oh, Lord, such innocent hopes! I may as well be just off the boat for all that's changed in twenty years!"

"Ella came from Austria, dear," my mother explained. "She studied with Freud."

Ella was quick to jump in. "No, no, dear. Never studied. *Was analysed* by one of his pupils. Which means only I *was discussed* over *kaffee* and *küchen*. The Perleman

Complex," she giggled. "No, I'm afraid I was too normal. I never made it into Freudian literature. You have heard perhaps of Freud, Philip?"

"Is it like a Freudian slip?"

"If you are not referring to a ladies' undergarment, yes, there is such a thing as a Freudian slip. You of course understand what this is — this Freudian slip as you call it?"

My mother was nodding fiercely, urging me on. What was it, a test? "Usually when you're talking and something dirty slips out accidentally. Or something embarrassing, like those radio bloopers. There's a nun in school I keep being afraid I'm going to call a *morse*, because that's her nickname."

"People always think Freud has to be dirty. Ah, well."

"You never told me about this nun, darling."

"What exactly is a *morse*, Philip?"

"You know, that big seal-like thing, with tusks."

"You mean a walrus, dear?" My mother's face looked stricken with pain, and she turned to Ella. "He's . . . you see?"

"Now, now. Mothers *worry*, don't they, Philip? It's perfectly all right to learn a second language. I've done it, many have done it."

"You were forced to," said my mother. "It's not like having your mother tongue taken from you. They won't let him speak English. I'm the only person he can speak English with."

Dolly came in from the kitchen, bearing a teapot on a silver tray, four fine china cups and a plate of biscuits around a jar of lemon curd. She lifted a lavender shawl off the teapot and Ella asked me, "Do you know what this is called, Philip?"

"A cover?"

"A cosy. A tea-cosy. Very strange word, I always thought."

"I like lemon curd," I said, emphasizing those last two words. "I don't see why it's called lemon curd. It's more like lemon pudding. I mean, milk gets curds. Curds and whey. Maybe because it's sour, but then why don't we have rhubarb curd and apple curd? Or do we? In French —" but I stopped myself.

"Dear," said my mother, "I'm sorry."

"English is not an especially logical language, Philip. As you have discovered. But tell me — are you enjoying yourself in Montreal? At school?"

"It's all right."

"Your mother tells me it's sometimes . . . a little primitive."

"They *beat* you, darling."

"They apologized. That's a big thing, getting them to apologize. La Morse herself, showed remorse." They didn't appreciate my rhyme. "It wasn't easy at the beginning even understanding things. Basic words, basic anything."

"What do you study?"

"It seems all he studies is Catholicism," said my mother.

The truth was, Apologetics was the easiest subject, since it required no thought, just memorization. It was also the quickest way to get good grades. The math was easier than Pittsburgh math, once I learned the number system. In Latin, though the text was in French, I was starting from the same place as other students. Given an even chance, I would always excel. "That's not true," I said. The truth, I realized, was unspeakable. The truth was, I *liked* Apologetics. I spooned deeply in the curd pot and smeared it over a biscuit.

"So. A difference of perception, maybe?"

My mother took this as a rebuke. Her head sank. I wanted to console her, but instead helped Dolly drag over a dining-room chair.

Ella looked at my mother; she looked at Dolly; I helped myself to more lemon curd. Finally Ella asked, in a softer voice, "Do they make you go to Mass? Do they try to convert you?"

"I don't think so. I mean, everyone's Catholic, so they just assume I am too. I mean with a name like Carrier —" But I could see that, too, hurt my mother. "I mumble the prayers, but I don't go to Mass."

"You can go, dear. I don't want you to feel . . . different."

"I don't feel different," I said.

"Would you like to go to an English school?"

"I can't. My uncle —"

"Never mind about your uncle. Would you *like* to go to a good English school? The *best* English school? A private school?"

"I don't know."

"Philip, your mother and I and Dolly have discussed a plan. If you say yes, your mother will discuss it with your father. Dolly and I, we have no children. Probably there's a limit to the amount of charitable contributions I can make. You can live with us, and we will send you. I know professors, I know musicians, writers, artists. We go out every night, or we have people here who are the leaders not just of this city, not just this country —"

"— the *world*, darling. Ella is known all over the world."

"That's not the point. The point is, we want to share this — what should I call it? Power? Connection? Good fortune? You could stay here in your own room and go home on the week-ends, of course. You would be prepared for McGill. I don't know what else there is to say."

"Say you will think about it, dear."

"I don't think my mother really wants me to leave," I said.

"She is the one who brought it up. She is deeply worried, what is happening to you."

"Nothing is happening to me."

"She wants what is best. French schools in this city are, well, substandard."

Inwardly, I panicked. There seemed to be no way of saving myself from everyone's good intentions.

"Before it's *too late*, darling. Before you lose everything you've got. They'll take it from you, believe me," and her voice suddenly cracked and her head fell to Ella's lap and I could hear the words torn from her chest. "Like . . .they've . . .taken . . . it . . . from . . . me!"

Ella took little note of the distraction; she placed her hand in my mother's hair and said to me, coldly and evenly, "Guess, please, Philip, how many products of classic French Canadian education we have on the McGill faculty. Go ahead."

I knew that any answer would be humiliating. "Obviously," she said, "you've guessed correctly. How many French Canadian *students* do you think I have?" She waited. "Let me tell you a little parable about the power of education. On this continent at the present time there are approximately six million French Canadians — am I right?"

"Yes," I admitted. It depended on how you counted our lost brothers and sisters in the West, New England and Louisiana. I'd just been reading about them, grieving for them, in my history class. My palms were sweating, my neck hairs rising.

"And there are approximately five million Jews on this continent," she said. She smiled briefly. "End of parable. Do you understand what I am saying about education? Do they teach you *that* in French school? Do you know how the minds of those people have been *wasted*? How they continue to be wasted? Have they taught you anything about Freud?"

"No," I whispered.

"Einstein?"

"Back in Pittsburgh."

"Karl Marx?"

I felt a terrible pressure in my chest. It was the name that seemed to be hovering in the air all afternoon. All that talk of *the workers* and *the people* and the candidates who never got elected. There had been a cartoon circulated in school on the eve of the latest election: Karl Marx in a Santa suit, with "Parti Libéral" stencilled on his sack of toys.

"No!" I retorted.

"They're doing a splendid job of educating you, aren't they? You should be spending your time learning about science, politics, history, literature —"

"— and how to get electrocuted for being Russian spies?" I demanded.

My mother raised her head, and Ella stared back at me, hard, for several seconds. "Ella, I'm sorry —" my mother began, but Ella raised her hand, and my mother was silent. Dolly carried the tray back to the kitchen.

"I can't say I'm surprised," said Ella.

"I'm going back to school," I said. My mother reached out for me, imploring me to wait, we would all go to Murray's for lunch, but I thanked her, and the other women, for the lemon curd and tea, and wished them a pleasant lunch and a good afternoon.

There's a special light that strikes Montreal in April; a light so strong, so angled, that it bores through windows and the glass panels of apartment doors with the intensity of a projection beam. It acts like a magnifying lens, picking out cobwebs and dust motes, adding dimensions to the grain of wood, nubbiness to the sleekest fabric, seams and crannies to the tightest skin. The sidewalks resemble tidal basins with their residues of sand, and the snow is shrunk to black tongues of gritty ice, seeking shade. The walk home from school took a little longer, as I crushed little ice bridges over the swirling melt, and stood on rims of rounded ice till they snapped with a hollow thud and I could kick the chunks away. The days were longer, and even my tutorials with Thérèse ended in plenty of daylight. My grades were better than average, and the nuns' comments were even flattering. Nevertheless, Thérèse and I agreed that the tutoring should continue. Her English was far from perfect.

I think my mother found the courage, some time that winter, to keep calling Ella and to make their lunches a regular event. I was going downtown on my own, now that the weather had improved. Mick had come through with a job on St Catherine Street, just as he'd promised. I took over an old stand of his just up from the train station, handing out mimeographed leaflets of naked girls behind strings of balloons, naked girls with one leg up in a bathtub, naked girls doing just about anything, plus the offer of a free drink or free admission. It was cold work and a little seedy; Mick, as a trusted long-time employee, had been promoted to inside work with the props, nearer the girls. My job next year, if I proved reliable.

"Where's this place at, kid?" and it was a pleasure to direct the tourists in their language, to hear them mutter to their buddies just off the train, "Smart kid, you hear him?" and "Ask him if he has a sister." I learned to put on a touch of a Dollardish accent, to guarantee full credit for my linguistic accomplishment, and sometimes a little tip. I earned a quarter for every two hundred leaflets I passed, and a nickel for every one redeemed at the Club Lido.

Dollard had dropped out of school and gotten a job at Steinberg's, loading and delivering. Two of Théophile's sons-in-law got big jobs in the States, dry-walling for a motel chain, and suddenly our little apartment was filled with new appliances. Béatrice stored an automatic washing machine on the back gallery so that the hot soapy water could gush over the cars below. We got a television set, the first anyone had seen, even though Canadian television was barely launched, rudimentary. That didn't stop me from buying the wires and rigging some rabbit-ears and tying them to our chimney in an attempt to coax something, anything, from the air. Burlington, Plattsburgh — those towns that provided night-time English radio in my room — where were you when it really counted? Even KDKA in Pittsburgh came in, most nights.

There was talk of our moving out. My mother's old teaching licence was approved by the Protestant school board, but she didn't dare mention it in Théophile's house. Béatrice crossed herself whenever the word "Jew" entered the conversation, as it frequently did these days with Dollard's new employment; she might have thrown herself over the gallery at the mention of Protestants. My father looked for work, but he had to lie about previous employment — or find someone to lie for him. The future would always be insecure. I would hold up my hand against the glass of the front door, and April light passed through it like X-rays. The tangle over where to live and where to send me would flare again in the summer, and the fall could be another disaster. I studied my skeleton on the door while the grunts and curses and cleaning sounds passed in the air around me.

Everyone had a few hours to themselves on Sunday afternoon, after the Mass and big meal. We dressed for the meal, and even Dollard managed some pleasantness for the few hours it took. I kept him supplied with free-drink passes at the Club Lido. Thanks to Mick, I even got in a few hours' work backstage, drew close to undressed women, heard and understood all their complaints. I told my mother those nights I was at the Forum, standing for hockey.

Those warming Sunday afternoons Thérèse and I would meet at the trolley stop nearest her apartment, and if the weather was nice we'd walk to Parc LaFontaine. We had a bet: she'd read two English books for every French book I read. It wasn't fair; she'd discovered Nancy Drew and the Hardy Boys while I slogged through Claudel and St-Denys-Garneau. She was doing well, she had wonderful discipline. And on Sundays she wore her church-going, dinner-eating dress and earrings, and she was a marvellous sight. Once, a priest walked by; she stiffened, but he smiled down at us and chuckled, "*Ah, jeune Montréal!*" She made me ashamed of the money I earned working the train station; I spent all of it I could on her.

By May we could walk all the way downtown if we wanted. May in Montreal is like April in Paris; the light is more forgiving, the haze of green is everywhere and the schoolwork, despite nuns' warnings, starts to relent. I remember a Sunday in May as though it is borne to me now on the laser beams of April light, imprinted and never to be forgotten. Walking down St Catherine Street with Thérèse O'Leary. We went to Murray's, and she'd taken my hand as we walked out. I'd ordered and paid in English, and she'd been terribly impressed. She'd promised me she'd do it, but had gotten too embarrassed at the last moment. We were walking behind a group of old ladies in white gloves and wide-brimmed hats, the tea-drinking ladies of Westmount, and Thérèse had been frightened of them, afraid of what they might be saying about her. Just gossip, I said, mindless things, and I translated some of it, to reassure her. She shook her head and acted ashamed. "*Sh'peux pas!*" she declared, pounding the side of her head with her fists, "*Idiote!*", then giggled. "*Mais tu peus, non?* You hunnerstan' every word, non? Smart guy!" She took my hand in both of hers and swung my arm like the clapper of the biggest bell in th world.

Translation

Translation

1

At forty-three, Porter, *né* Carrier, feared he was sick again. The warning came at night with a vision and an odour just as it always had. Debbie suspected nothing. She was mincing tuna for a week's supply of sandwiches. He loved the sound of a long silver spoon knocking the sides of an empty mayonnaise jar.

He said, "For the first time in my life, I really know that I'm going to die. It's a profound awareness."

She didn't look up. "Am I disagreeing?" She'd been spending most weekends with him for the past two years. She would soon be thirty.

"It's the way you're looking in that bowl."

"Philip, how do you *want* me to look into a bowl of tuna fish? Let me translate what you're saying. You're saying that you read in a paper today that someone who meant the world to you when you were fourteen years old just died." She looked up, smiling wickedly for confirmation. "You're the proverbial ear in the forest, don't you know? The one that actually hears every tree that falls? It's okay, Porter, it's okay to die."

"You'll find more mayonnaise in the pantry."

"If every man's death diminished me the way it does you — God, I'd disappear!" She licked mayonnaise off her knuckles. "But you don't actually diminish, do you? You're no anorexic. I'm sure you grieve in your way, but it keeps you going."

As much as Porter loved her most days, he knew the relationship was ending. Not because of her reaction, which was appropriate. It was ending because of the vision.

Dying had been a spectacle, something older people did for his pity or instruction. Death had been mowing down the radio greats of his childhood and the holdover politicians of the New Deal, then the actors his parents had thrilled to and the boys of his happiest summers when he'd been a child and they'd been in their prime. And now there was no gap left. He'd sung their songs, thrilled to their debuts, made love to them in his dreams. He'd been standing at the end of a long queue, bored by how slowly it moved, but now the soft shuffle of the quotidien had taken him to the ticket stand and the open doors of a darkened theatre.

"People I've loved are dying," he said.

"Porter, dear, you have many lovable traits. But please don't tell me you know what it is to love." She smeared two Ry-Krisps with tuna salad. "Not that it matters."

He'd heard it often enough. Until Amy, his first wife, left, Porter had thought himself a deprived, embittered man capable of great tenderness. She taught him he was a sophisticated lover from a privileged background, lacking none of the graces except a core of essential decency.

2

His childhood dream had been of a glacier, or at least of something cold, mountainous and inexorable bearing down on him. He could hear and even see through its gelatinous distortions the grinding of boulders and forests, and he could smell the scorched, catastrophic swath of natural pavement in its path.

He would wake, often screaming. It moved a foot a year, and he couldn't outrun it. He always woke when the ice touched him with its scalding cold. When flesh met glacier they were fused, like tongue to an ice tray.

His mother would be holding him and by then extracting the wooden spoon she kept at his bedside. He would bury his aching head in her breast, and she would hold him, swaying.

"The glacier again?" and he would nod. "See, there's nothing out there." He wouldn't open his eyes. After those attacks colours were too bright to bear, and the odours of the world all bordered on rottenness. It was as though life were offering a putrefied version of itself for his eyes and nose only.

Those were the attacks at night in sleep. In the day his nose would fill with a sweet, burnt odour, and colours would turn red like ageing film and kids would say, "Hey, Porter, I'm talking to you!" Sometimes he'd find himself on the floor or on the ground, his muscles numb from supreme exhaustion.

But all of that ended thirty years before.

Why now should life suddenly turn perilous? He went to his doctor for the first time in three years. Since his last visit he'd cut down his drinking to a few beers a week, had gum surgery and three crowns put in and lost thirty pounds. He jogged twenty miles a week and in the winter lifted weights and swayed to calisthenics. The doctor declared him 100 percent fit, a model of 1980s self-reclamation. America was seeing a generation of potential centagenarians.

"By the way," he asked, "what are you guys pushing for epilepsy?"

"Doing another story, Porter?" Porter had not been totally honest with his doctor. He'd never been honest with anyone. When he was forced into magazine writing between novels, he found the doctor an enthusiastic collaborator. He'd helped him with "Mid-Life to Mod-Life," "Toward a More Perfect Carcinogen," and his steroids piece, "Higher, Faster, Stronger . . . Dumber?"

"I'd heard that epileptic medicine can slow you right down to idiocy. If they'd treated Dostoyevski — no *Crime and Punishment*."

"No way," said the doctor. "Any new medicine comes on stronger at the beginning than it needs to be — look at the first birth-control pills, the Salk vaccine, the tranquillizers. The first generation anti-convulsants might have turned him into a zombie for a few weeks, but we'd have had him driving a car inside a month."

"That's very reassuring. And now?"

"Designer doses, Porter. Tegratol, Dilantin, some

phenobarb at night. We'd have nailed it. What are you writing?"

"I was thinking of giving a character a very heavy curse."

"Diabetes is good," the doctor mused. "Mainstream, too, with lots of paraphernalia. Or what about Huntington's Chorea? That can *really* ruin your day." Porter's doctor conferred imaginary disorders with greater enthusiasm than ever went into their healing.

"Let me get back to you," he said.

3

One day Debbie was making tuna salad and inviting him to parties, and a few weeks later she was busy in Manhattan with her children. A month after that she announced she wanted to go to Europe for spring break, alone.

He wasn't even disappointed. In marriage most men are tempted early and often by other women. Porter loved women, but his great temptation was solitude. Amy had called him a libertine monk. Debbie left him in February. Snow was deep; he doubled his calisthenics and benchpresses and set August as the date for the delivery of his novel. After five earlier books of stories and two novels with childhood and adolescent characters, this was to be his wet-winged emergence into the adult world of marriage and poisonous self-knowledge. He was not unhappy, in his bitter, private way, that no one would be interfering with his ridiculous little schedules.

He lived in a cottage in Duchess County. Amy had kept

their old house in Binghamton, their kids were on scholarship, and with a pasta diet, a garden and few vices, he could just about live on his writing. The nearest town was Poughkeepsie, where Debbie taught. He went into New York when he had good reasons.

According to many who knew him, Porter wasn't altogether sane. He'd been a professor, then had changed jobs, surrendered tenure, taken pay cuts and finally come to the conclusion — logical under the circumstances — that the remaining obligations were too strenuous, underpaid and insecure to keep at all. He taught for a while as an adjunct in metropolitan campuses with "at" in their titles. The self-destruction had cost him a marriage.

During the February thaw, the dripping icicles and the hiss of wet tires on the exposed blacktop outside the cottage lured him into three days of bonus running. He valued the accretion of small details and the web of images that clung to him as he ran. He loved the things of this world, passionately. He loved activities like running that stimulated a disinterested scrutiny. Running was like writing a short story, a familiar habit begun in pain but ending breathless and exultant. Weight-lifting, so dramatically exerting, so ambitious, was like writing novels.

As he ran that first day looking at the early buds on the trees and hedgetips, he realized he couldn't name a single tree in English. He'd probably never known them in French — there hadn't been many trees in his life as a Carrier. They all existed in some abstraction of treeness. He was a writer, after all, and to name was to know. All he knew for certain was childhood in Pittsburgh and adolescence in Montreal, plus some articles aided by a doctor's vocabulary.

He smelled it again, a putrescence in the world, as though a winter's worth of carcasses had been shovelled to the roadside.

He took three days off for a trip to the city, uncharacteristically, to check out the movies and bookstores. When he got back to his typewriter, the novel was cold.

4

Thirty years before when he'd been X-rayed at Pittsburgh General, the neurologist had termed his epilepsy "trauma-induced," meaning that a childhood injury — a skull fracture at the age of three — was the probable cause. And with adolescence the skull might achieve adult contour, and he could be free of seizures for the rest of his life.

It had returned a day or two after the thaw. He'd been writing in bed — still his position for serious work — when he'd noticed a puddle of coffee on his sheets and the mug overturned in the blanket. The coffee was almost cold.

He'd known many people like himself — arrested cancer victims, one-time cardiac patients, recovered alcoholics — who'd mastered the etiquette of daily gratitude. They never planned, they never deferred. Gratitude had never been Porter's style, but he heard himself praying over the coffee stains, *Please, God, don't let it come back. Let me finish this one last book, that's all I ask.*

In response, God pinged him lightly a second time. Like mice and returned cheques, seizures came in clusters.

The medicine he'd taken all his childhood had made him slow. It hadn't been until his rebirth as Philippe Carrier in Montreal that the curse had disappeared. His high school had classified epileptics with the insane and retarded. There'd been a girl, Marie Bolduc, nicknamed *la tordue*, who'd been taken around to classes strapped in her wheelchair where she sometimes slumped and stiffened ten times an hour. Her neck was one enormous muscle. The sisters never caned her, despite her blatant disruptiveness and frequent inattention, though they were not above using her as an example of God's wrath, or His mercy.

She'd been the first death in his life, the first of his generation to go under. Laid out to her full length in the open casket, neck cushioned against the satin, she'd been a tall, pretty girl. Some of his classmates had snickered, half-expecting the coffin to give a sympathetic lurch. He'd snickered louder than any of them.

When he returned to his novel after that seizure and the memory of a distant funeral Mass (having epilepsy, he'd once written of a character, was like writing with a ballpoint pen that occasionally skipped), his arm was numb, his fingers cold and tingling, and he found it immensely hard to catch up with his thoughts. He remembered perfectly the gelatinous, unresponsive, mental fatigue of epilepsy. He remembered feeling like a human glacier, an obstruction, slow and brutish. In the depths of his brain he could smell fresh ironing, and he caught a glimpse of a woman in a bathrobe who disappeared before he could recognize her.

When he next looked at his novel, it was dead. He didn't recognize the writing, he couldn't even imitate it. He turned a page and wrote three sentences that had nothing to do with anything he'd ever written:

> The sons of suicides bear a graceless burden. She let go of my hand as the bus approached. "There's something I must do," she said, and pulled away.

5

And so it was not to be the novel that made Porter relatively rich and famous; it was *Head Waters*, an autobiography. During his years as a professor he'd often lectured on autobiography, calling it a maligned and poorly described art form that attracted more than its share of hacks. "The self-biographers," he'd termed them, those who saw their own lives as miniature histories, who began their books with the fatal words, "I was born . . . " as though life had not existed before them, and the glory and pain of self-consciousness — the true subject of all autobiography — were not finding the niche where one fit, but clearing a site for the shopping-mall of the self. Porter called autobiography the democracy of bafflement. Every success reinvented the form.

He refused all medication while he wrote. He was forced to spread pillows under his chair. He glued a strip of foam rubber to the metal rim of his typewriter, and he gave up trying to drive.

Because he even feared walking into the village for food (twice he'd fallen, spilling his groceries, and once he'd wakened to see tire tracks across his loaf of bread), he took in a woman. Her name was Petra, a middle-European who assisted in Vassar's Russian program. She was forty and had never married. Sex between them was infrequent and barely satisfying. Porter felt himself diminishing as a man, disappearing into his infirmities and literary graces. He made love like an old man seeking comfort. From one of those early encounters, Petra got pregnant. Porter counselled abortion (half-heartedly; his soul was deeply Catholic), and in their second year Petra and his daughter stayed week-ends and came over twice a week.

Hannah was an old-fashioned little girl: wide-eyed, well behaved, Old World. Even as a pre-toddler she sat on the breakfast table while her mother cooked, playing with silverware and paper plates, never dropping them on the floor, never straying over the edge. Her isolation and intensity frightened him. He thought, "Hanno Buddenbrooks," and felt she was doomed, a dead end, the last Carrier, the last Simonovska. She had taken her mother's name. He'd resigned his role in this second family. He doubted he'd live much beyond her early schooling.

Petra never intended marriage or motherhood. Yet in some strange and uncharacteristic way, he had *courted* her. She had arrived as a companion, a cook, a driver; he had forced the issue. She mentioned that her previous experiences with men were less frequent than those with women, but her deepest drives were, like his, private, studious, uncommunicative.

He wondered if Hannah would grow up to reflect on the absurdity of her birth, that in a normal world she would never have been. She owed her life to his epilepsy. Would it shock her? Amuse her? She was a child of accident and calculation; she never cried, never whined, took delight in spoons and glasses and started violin and piano lessons before she was three. She stared at the world like an intent Anne Frank, with a face perfectly composed and adult. Even if he was forced to leave her early he could see exactly how she'd look twenty years down the line.

6

Some time in his forty-fifth year Porter asked his body, "Okay, what do you want? What are you trying to tell me?"

He'd been studying his face in the bathroom mirror. Of course he'd aged, lost weight, and his hair and whiskers were greying. But it was the cuts, the scabs, the myriad nicks and tiny bruises he suddenly noticed; like a drunk's. The dozens of small stumblings, the sprains and burns and confused looks from everyone but Petra that indicated to him he was having more episodes than he'd even suspected. The ballpoint pen was running out of ink.

An interviewer came over from Boston, and Porter must have blanked out in the middle of a question. When he'd come out of it the interviewer was saying to his sound man, "We'll go back to where I ask, 'Why did you leave Montreal and return to the United States?' " And to Porter he'd asked matter-of-factly, "Would you like a glass of water?"

Porter, still confused, had mumbled, "Montreal can break your heart."

But now his body was giving no answers. "My head's shrinking, is that it?" The skull was closing in ever so slightly. There had to be a message in it. In rational, pain-free moments he caught glimpses of his disease like a shadow leaving the room the second he snapped on a light. He could almost catch it, almost smell it (the smell of ironed clothes turned sour), and once or twice alone in his cottage he heard himself shouting, "Stop, you!" and his mind tried to lock on the shadow. It was *possession*, wasn't it, just as the ancients and the conjurers had always said — a devil to be cast out. At least that was one alternative.

Once in his teen years in Montreal, an orphan living with whores and working in a strip joint, young Carrier had dragged himself to a free clinic, complaining of fatigue, weight loss, stomach pains, bleeding and worst of all, *a sense of evil*. The nun had taken down the symptoms, pausing a while on *malaise globale*, but otherwise moved by his distress and orphaned state.

"Where do you live?" the doctor had asked.

"Around," he'd answered, not wishing to compromise the janitors who let him sleep in basements and the girls who gave him food and a bed in their off-hour mornings. Those had been his *célinesque* years in Montreal, when the city had finally made sense to him.

The doctor was listening to his stomach. "What are you eating?"

"Whatever I can get," he'd answered. Waitresses would sneak it out. He was only seventeen.

The doctor seemed to be addressing the nun. "I would say this young man is harbouring a serpent in his bowels." Then he turned to Carrier. "A worm, understand, young man? You may well have thirty feet of tapeworm swimming around down there — no wonder you're weak and bleeding. Its head is chewing into your stomach, and by now it's taking four-fifths of everything you eat. And it's *still* not satisfied. So we'll feed it a little something extra."

Carrier's complaint was not uncommon in the slum clinics of Montreal in the mid-fifties. The doctor had free samples in his drawer, and the effects, he warned, would be dramatic.

"If you are in the habit of gazing fondly at your stool, I would strongly advise against it for the next three weeks," he said.

Porter, remembering the chunks of the beast as they passed through him, thought again of purgation, and something in his deeply Catholic soul responded. *I've got you, you bastard*. He tapped his temple. *You can run, but you can't hide*. He put away his razor blade — no use taking chances — he'd let his beard grow out, white or not. He looked into his eyes so closely he could almost see the beast behind them.

Hiding, are you?
I'm taking you home, baby.

7

Porter dreaded the Canadian border. The simplest questions of an immigration officer were the imponderables of his life: What is your name? Where were you born? What is your nationality? If Porter had a demon in his brain, taking it to Montreal was like poking a stick in its cage. He didn't have a passport and couldn't get one. Canada was the world for Porter; America was all there was for Carrier.

Head Waters had been a success in several languages. Philippe Carrier's *Les Sources de mémoire* had been a local best-seller for Les Éditions d'aujourd'hui. They'd wanted him to go on the talk shows in Montreal, but he'd refused. "Ah, we understand, M'sieur Carrier," the publisher had said. "We're very small, and we can't afford to pay you well." It wasn't that, but better they thought it was. The simple truth was that he was an illegal alien, just as his father had been, and sooner or later, given publicity, questions would be asked.

Often he'd had to rehearse his border crossings. He'd work on his accent, seeking to match it to his New York plates and licence. In his bus-riding years, he would go up to Montreal as fun-loving Phil Porter, and return to the States as humble Carrier, down to visit a cousin. He was always afraid the officer would ask him first, "Where were you born?" instead of "Where do you live?"

Phil Porter, in reality, did not exist. No such person had ever been born. "Porter" had been his father's fiction, easily dropped when cornered (*coincé*, in fact, was his father's favourite word), but Porter had been trapped in it. Like any threatened faith, it now seemed all the more precious. He held an American social security card under one name and a Canadian social insurance card under another. It was a complicated little drama, but one that suited him. For this trip in the summer of his forty-sixth year he'd flown in as Phil Porter, Expos fan, for a week of baseball.

This isn't my city, he told himself in the airport bus. *It was Carrier's city. It's all an accident.* Let it go. False intimacies can kill. Acknowledged attachments bring only bills and sentimental cards on Father's Day. Bills he willingly paid for the privacy they bought.

The infinite perversity of life — as the nuns would say — that the sincere involvements undertaken with a dream of permanence, marriage and fatherhood, had deserted him. Only the coldest and most brutal, Petra and Hannah, showed any sign of lasting. And one other. One other chunk of flesh that inhabited his body and possessed his mind *still*. Porter, a man of few attachments, was haunted by unbearable intimacies. Even a French rock station listened to by a Haitian taxi-driver lit cells in Porter that were floodlights in Carrier's cave.

8

He met Florence Lachance, the publicist for his publisher, in a small Lebanese restaurant in a remodelled area behind the Main. It was a hot day, and she wore a T-shirt and jeans, with the publisher's logo over her modest bosom. Across her back was a picture of his book. It didn't concern him.

"They've loved it," she said, riffling through a packet of reviews. He was called, in a casual translation, not quite a cultural chameleon, more a . . . what? Newt? Mud-puppy? Thanks a lot.

"They're calling you a new Kerouac," she went on. "There's a word they use at the university — *porterisme* — for a kind of special Quebec tragedy."

He read a long review more closely. To its author he was an intermediate cultural life-form, not slimy by intention like Monsieur Trudeau, not a cultural chameleon like the Ottawa mandarins, but a permanent, arrested cultural larva with lungs for land and gills for water.

She watched him frown and reached across to tap his hand. "Oh! Not *you*, M'sieur Carrier. It's the *situation* you describe. Ten years ago people would have said it's what happens when you're just a colony. They would have called you *vendu*. Now they see we're all like . . . those things. I can't say the word."

"Axolotls," he said. He thought: I *am* my condition.

She giggled. She looked so chagrined he wanted to hold her. The role of publicist for a Quebec publishing house seemed so cosy and absurd, so *sincere* and guileless, that he felt light-headed with remorse.

He glanced at the first sentence.

Les fils des suicides supportent un fardeau sans grâce.

"Who's this Madeleine Choquette?"

Florence squinted and asked, "Seriously? Madeleine Choquette?" As though he'd asked, Who's this Wayne Gretzky character?

"She begged us to let her do you. You'll meet her."

"A writer, then?"

"One of the important writers. She's also very well known in France. People compare your book with hers all the time — maybe you don't like that? Do they ask you that — why you don't come back? Why you don't write in French?"

"All the time," he said, lying graciously. No one in the States knew or cared that he'd had a double life. Most Americans couldn't really conceive of it, and most of those who did couldn't conceive of its being French Canadian. They were talking in French, but his French, he wanted to say, wasn't good enough. It had once been a thin, elastic membrane, transparent and stuffed with words. Now it was a loose sack of familiar phrases, a duffel bag to drag along on trips to Montreal. *Fardeau* or *charge*? *Supporter* or *appuyer*? What's wrong with good old *porter*, "to carry"? Hell would be having to make a conscious choice, like a translator, between dozens of perfectly serviceable likenesses for every phrase of every sentence.

He could tell, looking at her in her blue-tinted glasses, at her confused little frown and her nervous way with a cigarette, that she'd asked another question while he'd ducked under his unspeakable little cloud.

"Can I get you anything?" she whispered.

"Now you know something else about me. Not just an axolotl, but an axolotl with epilepsy."

A familiar path doubling over. He wondered if he was doomed to enter a violent convulsive stage, as he had when he was eleven and twelve back in Pittsburgh. Would he be driven all the way back to the battering when he was three, was he doomed to repeat it all?

She recovered graciously. "We have an interview with Corinne Carrier at Radio-Canada. You'll like her, and she knows Madame Choquette. She'll introduce you, M'sieur Carrier."

Carriers and Smiths, thought Porter. Everything in Quebec was sooner or later connected, everyone eventually related. So much so that the names were interchangeable, like Changs. Only a fool or a foreigner would assume an actual, blood connection.

9

In the buried years that Carrier had lived in his uncle Théophile's flat, his cousin Dollard, two years older, had been his window on an intolerable future. Dollard had dropped out of school at fourteen and worked at a series of manual jobs, digging and filling, until Théophile's political and church connections had gotten him on the city payroll. He was sent to work as a *fossoyeur* at Côte-des-Neiges Cemetery, the Vatican City of digging and filling. By that time, Carrier and his parents had left Théophile's flat and found a smaller one of their own a few miles west in Snowden. His father sold kitchen equipment in a restaurant-supply house on the Main. His mother had started substitute teaching in the Protestant schools all over the western parts of the island.

And then his father disappeared. Not exactly vanished — he first got in practice by making himself scarce. He would come home to sleep in the middle of the week, but wouldn't show up on weekends. Fishing, he said, or hunting, knowing that his wife didn't approve of either, or the men he did it with. Then he disappeared altogether.

Carrier and his mother moved into two rooms near McGill. She wanted him to transfer to a Protestant English school before his French Catholic allegiance cost him his soul, and her job. "Before it's too late," she always put it, but he fought her. He was sixteen; the brothers wanted him to go to Laval.

One day after school young Carrier took a trolley over to the restaurant-supply store. It was a Jewish place, but the men inside spoke every language on the Main. His father spoke a pretty fair Yiddish, perfect Italian and adequate Greek and Portuguese. He could even make Armenians and Lebanese feel at home. Carrier *fils* had won a

Latin prize at school, and he wanted to show it to his father. But Mr Samelowitz said Carrier *père* hadn't been working there for months. Something unpleasant, but he wouldn't go into it. For as long back as Carrier could remember, people had spoken of his father in hushed, embarrassed tones. Where he had gone, no one knew, or would tell. That's how it remained.

He tried to remain faithful to both families, as much as Montreal etiquette permitted. They were now living on the English side of town — which Théophile equated with wealth and perfidy — though no one around them spoke a word of English or had a dime to their name. If his father was in touch with them, they never mentioned it. Nevertheless, he had attended Dollard's wedding three years later, in Longueil. The wife, Paulette, he remembered as another small, squat, beetle-browed addition to a family already overrun with cultural clichés. At the time, she was three months pregnant. And there *had* been a daughter, he recalled, born the following spring, twenty-five years ago. And he remembered her name as Corinne.

Quebec might be twice the size of Texas, but its people were all one family. In a family of five million there are bound to be thousands of Corinne Carriers; hundreds, perhaps, with parents by the name of Dollard and Paulette. Still, it was possible. It was a culture made for coincidence.

One look at Corinne Carrier seemed to confirm an utter lack of common ancestry, for which Porter, ever on the lookout for new love, gave silent thanks. She was the right age for cousinhood — twenty-five — but too tall, too beautiful, with long, greying hair, a rectangular face with large green eyes and a generous mouth. The classic Carrier face was just the opposite: small features pulled chinward like a cod's. He associated her kind of charm with ageing stars of the French cinema — not quite beautiful, but so animated they turned nearby men into unwitting cameras. She wore a thirsty satin blouse and faded jeans with beaded moccasins. She moved and spoke with expensive, inherited grace. Her French was Radio-Canada International, without the pouting, asphyxiating gutterals of Paris.

Her show was called *"Quelques paroles pour l'après-midi,"* or more familiarly, *"Corinne t'en parle."* Bright tapestries from Asia or Africa were hung on her dressing-room walls. Interspersed were dozens of framed black-and-white stills taken from movies. *Her* movies. She took him on a tour of her walls.

"We were shooting in Cuba last year," she explained. "Those are from a documentary we made on child care in Cuba, Nicaragua and China."

There she stood with Castro, same height, her arm on his shoulder, looking chic and committed. She was a serious woman — another blow against consanguinity. Quebec had a long history of turning out flirts and strippers and kitteny bundles of winter delight, but something on the scale of Corinne? He'd have to go to Scandinavia to find her equivalent. A Quebec girl going to China? To Cuba! The girls he'd known had been lucky to get to Plattsburgh.

Porter asked if she had children — he was old enough now for avuncular questions — and she tossed off an amused shrug that told him her interests were feminist and political, not personal. "I'm only twenty-five, *please*, m'sieur!" In his Quebec, the only twenty-five-year-old unmarried women he'd known had been whores or nuns. One, in fact, Jeannine Jolicoeur, La Soeur Dure et Mure, had scandalized the eastern townships, stripping down to rosary beads from a nun's starched habit.

She took him into the radio studio, introduced him to Ree-shar, her sound man, a Gauloise-addicted, permed, tanned, but still pudgy man Porter's age, then sat him across from her behind a mike. They had a few minutes, but she was already in her interviewing mode, elbows on thighs, slumped forward, cleavage from the satin blouse as daunting as a *Cosmo* cover girl's. There was nothing on American television to touch her.

"I read your book last year as soon as it came out, of course, because of our connection. I thought it utterly remarkable. Frankly, I wasn't ready for those reviews, though! What did you think of them?"

What do I think of being a newt, an axolotl? He asked instead, "What connection?"

"Oh, don't tell me! — you don't know? I didn't think I had to tell you —"

"Not Dollard's daughter?"

"Of course. I've been hearing about you all my life. My father's brilliant cousin in America! When I started publishing my novels I even thought of sending them to you, but I figured you'd think it presumptuous. What if you hated them? What if you didn't want to hear from anyone up here? After all, you called yourself Porter."

"How could I think it presumptuous? If I'd known, it might have saved me." Her *novels*? Her films? Dollard's little girl? "I mean, I'm terribly out of touch."

"Who wouldn't be? It doesn't matter, you're out of the woodwork now, and *I'll* introduce you, starting tonight."

An old word leaped to mind, bringing a smile to his lips: *cousine de fesse gauche*. A kissing cousin. "So, frog begets princess," he said. How had any of this happened in just a generation? Mutations without a missing link.

"He wants to see you, by the way. He's alone — my mother's dead."

"We'll see."

"Where men still outlive women — that's backward," she said. "We've still got a long way to go. As you remind us, m'sieur." That seemed to be her cue to begin.

"I have just one request," he said. He tapped the glass, alerting Richard. "Put this show on a two-minute delay, okay?" Corinne frowned; she was all spontaneity.

"In case my French is rusty," he explained.

10

Corinne lived off St Denis near carré St-Louis. When he'd last inhabited the area it had been a low, squalid slum, dismal and tubercular. Post-war immigration and the diaspora from the old Jewish ghetto had made the area an attractive no man's land of suspect ethnicity between the once-solid halves of a bilingual city. And now, with the rest of the English nearly gone, the fulcrum had shifted further east, and the area was young, upscale, arty and French. Soho *de chez nous*, thought Porter. If he were ever to return to Montreal, as he sometimes fantasized, he too would settle near St Louis Square.

On a steamy night in July, Corinne and Richard threw a cocktail party in his honour. Alas, the pudgy little sound man in the tight polo shirt, jeans and gold chain was more than a sound man, and Porter had been slow in picking up the inflections.

Porter had been sipping beer in the kitchen, a lone, bushy-bearded, middle-aged man in shirtsleeves among men in abused leathers, cropped beards and baggy corduroys. Quebec was both chic and Third World at the same time; unlike New York, everyone smoked. The uncirculated summer air was dense and blue. It was like being in a Bogart movie, or something terribly earnest and existential.

He was the oldest male, but for two white-maned eminences from the upper levels of publishing. Richard came close, but worked at looking younger in his leather jacket, tight jeans, frizzy grey hair and tightly trimmed black beard. Culture matters, thought Porter; four hundred miles south of here and he'd look decked out for Fire Island or a cruise down Christopher Street.

He wondered why he'd let himself in for all this. Corinne was the only obvious reason, but Richard, if not older prohibitions, had blocked that possibility even before it arose. To meet his translator, perhaps. Or something older and more characteristic of him: to prove that even in a Montreal so utterly transformed he still had force, continuity. He didn't recognize any of the locally famous names, he'd read none of their books, he didn't know their films or plays or songs or the names of their publishing houses. He wanted to know if any of that really mattered. He wanted to prove to himself that he still had currency.

Richard had followed him to a small porch off the remodelled kitchen. They didn't seem to have much in common, beyond an obvious interest in Corinne.

"I listened very carefully to your interview this afternoon," Richard said, in the French they had been using together, then looked up slyly and added in English, "Right on, man!"

"Which part was right on?"

"Oh, the part about the perils of collective thinking. Or feeling a double loyalty and catching shit for not being loyal enough for either side. And not being able to explain *why* you feel so goddamned intense about your French Canadianness when there's at least six million just like you in New England who don't give a damn."

The man's English, at the very least, was remarkable. Not that it was unaccented, more or less like Corinne's, but that it was *noticeably* accented.

"And do you know what really broke me up? It was when Coco asked you such a simple little question as —"

"— *where was I born*? But that's not such a simple little question. I didn't know till I was thirteen, and it still gets me in trouble."

"Man, you turned white! It made my own hands sweat. I know *exactly* what you mean."

"Just where were you born, Richard?"

He snorted. "Shit, can't you tell? I didn't speak a word of *French* till I was twenty-three years old — that beats you by ten years. Look, do I sound *strange* or something?"

"You sound," said Porter, "like you learned your English in New York City."

"Well? You think *you* got identity problems? I grew up as Dick Goldstein in the Bronx. Came up here to dodge the draft, got a degree at McGill, got involved in anti-war stuff, then in PQ stuff, the independence thing, got married, had kids. Everybody's story."

"Except that now you're Ree-shar and you live with

Corinne Carrier. I'd call that life after death."

"And I've got two Jewish kids who went to French schools because that was the right thing to do, and now one's a folksinger in France and the other's a lumberjack on the North Shore and they both refuse to speak a word of English except when they sing. Try explaining *that* to their *zeyde* and *bubbe*. I did my six months for amnesty so I can at least go back and visit them."

"Have they met Corinne?"

"Sure. She freaks them out."

Porter could tell they'd gathered a small crowd behind him; he could smell the smoke of discovery. He could even detect the fragrance of his left-cheek cousin just at his elbow.

Richard winked and slipped back into French. "The Expos get back in town tomorrow, and I'm on the television crew. If you want to go, just get word to Coco."

That seemed to be her cue; she turned Porter with a touch on his shoulder. "M'sieur Carrier, there's someone here who's been wanting to meet you." An older woman in a pastel dress stepped forward. "May I present to you Madeleine Choquette, your translator? Madame Choquette, my cousin, Philippe Carrier."

11

Earlier in the evening he had noticed her, a stocky, grey-haired woman with youthful skin, and he'd assumed she was a publisher's wife. She had the assurance and the accessories that would have led anyone looking at her and Corinne together to think, "Of course!": mother and daughter. They made sense together. Maybe there hadn't been a mass mutation of the provincial gene-pool; parts of the Montreal generations really did fit together.

A flashbulb went off. Corinne moved automatically to the middle; the party had suddenly found its focus. He felt his translator's arm tighten around him, and he knew she had come alone. A young man wanted to know what he'd thought of the translation. He had to admit that he hadn't yet read it.

She said to him later, "Don't apologize, Mr Porter. Please, don't even bother reading it. In fact, you're the *last* person who should read it." Just as Florence Lachance had said, her English was perfect.

"You're the first person in Montreal to call me Porter."

"That's how I know you," she laughed. "And because you're no Carrier." She held out two fingers and pinched them just under his nose. "We're *this* close, you and me. But I'm on one side and you're on the other, and no one but you or me could tell us apart."

"So what does that make me?"

"An American. A Franco-American. Like the spaghetti."

Just when he was getting used to being a newt, an axolotl.

It was a warm night, still early. Corinne's apartment opened on a pedestrian mall lined with restaurants and bistros. Somewhere on these streets that were now closed to traffic, young Carrier had lived with whores, had slept on their sofas, gotten up at noon and made his way to the backs of unsanitary restaurants where part-time hookers, the sisters of strippers, the girl-friends of various petty gangsters and enforcers on the block, served him food. By afternoon he'd show up on Dorchester Street where he had a job sweeping and mopping at the Club Lido. Fifi Laflamme, *née* Jeanne Gobeil, had been a headliner, and there was Kitty Coulombe who worked with doves and Soeur Cerise, too outrageous even for Montreal. And every night there'd been a circle of men around the horseshoe stage slurping drinks and reaching up for a feel, whom Carrier zapped with imaginary death rays as he worked the reds and purples. He could remember it all perfectly tonight, the girls, the smells and the twisted alleys off rue de Bullion, the steamy nights of unscreened windows and the ice-etched glass of winter with pans of water on the rads, the girls waiting in front of the *cassescroûtes* for Americans dropped off by taxi-drivers.

He was seventeen and dreaming of purity, living in the midst of sin and disease. The girls had TB, they had social diseases ("Honey, I'd let you climb on 'cause I really like you, but I'm doing you a favour, see?"), they had little kids that Carrier would take to the park on nice days while their mothers slept.

Why *can't* I forget all this?

He'd written about those years. He'd squeezed it all out, but he was still tortured. It was all so Catholic, so medieval, he was a four-hundred-year-old man. He remembered trying to sleep on a torn sofa as Félice Gagnon stood under sixty punishing watts, not his forgiving reds and blues, ironing a dress. She'd stand there for hours half-dressed in a pair of black undies as he buried himself in the crooks of her sofa.

Tonight with his translator in Montreal he felt as though he'd been reduced to a burst of static and flung into space for thirty years, and only now, with this woman, finally captured. He wanted to trust her, this woman so close to him in fate but from the other side of the world. They had a small second dinner at a Greek seafood restaurant, fried squid, salad, retsina.

He'd often wondered, back in his married days, and in his years with Debbie, what it would take to make a healthy, vigorous, attractive man ever grow interested in an older woman. Even if he *ought* to. Even if it was the best thing for him, not to mention the right political thing to do? It just seemed unnatural. And now he knew that unblemished young women were merely the least complicated form of a polymorphous attraction.

Of course, he was no longer healthy, young or vigorous.

"I want to hold you," he said.

"Of course you do," said his translator. "And you will."

12

These were dangerous streets for Porter, the steep downtown slopes between MacGregor and Sherbrooke — Peel, Stanley, Drummond, Mountain — for it was in a tourist room between Burnside and St Catherine on Peel that young Carrier had last lived with his mother. After seeing Madeleine home (a woman of a certain age leads a complicated life, she reminded him; he could not visit her *that* night, but was welcome the next morning), Porter had walked back down Park from Outremont to the complex around Pine, then down the rest of the mountain to Sherbrooke.

It had been Peel Street in 1956, before Montreal joined the twentieth century. No Métro, no autoroutes, no democracy, no self-expression outside of stripping and skating. Carrier and his mother had two rooms. She still went by the name of Hennie Porter; otherwise questions would arise. In the winter, she would leave before dawn for her teaching assignment. He would take off in his coat and tie for the *collège* on Côte-Ste-Catherine across from the Oratory. And when he got back his mother would still be gone, and he'd change clothes and walk down to the Club Lido. His mother thought he was selling programs at the Forum. He remembered that year, even now, as a happy time.

She was fifty-two, an attractive woman with dark hair and bold, non-Carrier features. She surprised people by her age. Education and travel kept her young, she said — she didn't know what people did in this life without memories of better times. She'd studied and worked in Europe and held responsible decorating jobs in Montreal before getting married. She should never have married, she said, though she didn't regret motherhood. That was her matrimonial refrain.

The schizophrenic twenties and thirties had formed her. She doodled flappers on the backs of envelopes, sketched Art Deco interiors, hung pictures of Shaw and Huxley. But she'd been in Germany for the rise of Hitler, been forced from the Bauhaus to Prague, from Prague to Warsaw, Warsaw to London and London finally to Montreal. Thanks to his mother, Carrier learned — long before he could ever use it in dead, repressive Montreal

— that once upon a time there had been a human place of sublime achievement against which the accomplishments of North America were to be held accountable and owing.

She was also a gloomy reactionary, cynical and suspicious. She attracted men without much effort — Carrier was an expert, reading lust in the eyes of strangers — but her only friends were mannish couples of unmarried women. She had married in her early thirties and suffered his father's instability and constant infidelities.

In 1956, Carrier was living in three discrete worlds: that of his mother and a cultured, English-speaking world focused on McGill University; that of a scholarship boy at an elite French *collège*, and that of a janitor in a bilingual shrine to venereal veneration. He was choking on female intimacy. The celibate world of the *collège* was his island of relief from a sea of powders, creams and endless costuming. He led a life of pure disguise; if the brothers had discovered his job, he would have been dropped from school. If the Protestant school board knew he attended a French Catholic school, his mother would have been fired. If his mother ever found out where he worked, she would have died. If he'd acted on any of his passions, he would have been arrested.

He and his mother had evolved an elaborate sexual etiquette. In matters of modesty, she was not of this century. They neither spoke of sex, nor alluded to any of its forms. They kept all doors locked even during the mildest states of disarray.

Then one day he'd come home from school and found his mother in the bathroom with the door open. She was preparing for her bath. She stood before the mirror in her dressing-gown and was busy brushing out her hair. He made as much noise as he could, and she turned to face him. "Hello, dear, did you have a good day?" she asked, perkier than usual, then unknotted the bow and spread her arms, and the robe fell open. He'd expected a joke to save him at the last minute, like the girls at the Lido, a slip at least, but her body had engulfed him, white, close, utterly, utterly nude. His legs went rubbery. "I'll go —" he said, and she answered him, stepping out of the bathroom and moving towards him, "No, it's quite all right. We're two adults here, aren't we? Why don't you put some tea water on?" and he ran for the kitchen cubicle while the rings of the shower curtain scraped against the rusty pole.

He stood in the kitchen watching the gas rings, hands moist and shaking, eyes burning from the vision. It was as though the gas had sucked all the air out of the room and the pounding of the water and the echoes off the bathroom tiles were in the kitchen with him. He could hear it all again tonight, nearly thirty years later, and his breath still came short.

When he had dared to turn, holding out the cup of tea, she was unwrapping herself from the towel in order to dry her hair. An alien being had occupied her body. "Just put it down, dear," she said, as she took a chair and finished drying her legs and thighs.

13

One day in the winter of his sixteenth year, Philippe Carrier had been a scholarship student at Jean-de-Brébeuf with a bright future before him in law or the classics, and the next day he'd been clawed from the skies and dumped in the gutter with nowhere to turn. He'd been standing with his mother at seven-thirty in the morning on the corner of Peel and Dorchester where the buses came in. She wasn't going to work that day, but she'd wanted to walk with him to the bus stop. She'd been bright and witty, her twenties not her thirties self, full of brittle talk and saucy opinion — the side he preferred, but couldn't fully respond to. It was easier to be the son of her sour, schoolteacherly side.

It had been a mushy morning in late March, with the night's fresh snow already crushed to slabs of silvered sherbet by the pre-dawn plows and now the rows of backed-up buses. Twenty different bus lines circled Dominion Square; buses were lined two abreast in the street and bumper-to-bumper along the curb. It was the sign of late winter, his mother observed, the number of lone male galoshes poking up from the puddles, sucked off by slush.

His bus, an express, sent up a wave of brown, salted ice as it slanted to its dock. Carrier was looking down at his feet, making sure of his footing, when his mother took his hand and said, "There's something I must do," and then pulled away and dove for the right front tire. The driver slammed his brakes so hard he mounted the curb, but his mother had already disappeared under the bus in the slushy, black pool of gutter water. A woman screamed at Carrier, "*Qu'est-ce que c'est passé?* — What happen'?" and he found himself pushed aside by policemen and drivers and some passengers who worked their way under the bus to pull his mother out.

At the inquiry it was determined that she must have slipped on the icy curb and been pushed forward by the surging crowd. Carrier did not dispute the finding, and for thirty years he'd accepted it. He concealed from everyone the letters she had left back in their rooms: a termination notice from the Protestant school board and, from the nearest town in Ontario, a notice from his father to file a Bill of Divorcement since Quebec did not permit divorces.

He was now standing at the spot. In front of him now was a six-lane Dorchester Boulevard and just down the hill the giant cheese-grater known as the Château Champlain Hotel. Windsor Station and the old Laurentian Hotel, profitable places for passing out peep-show leaflets, and the old Club Lido itself were gone, and Dominion Square was now an art park. The only survivors he could place from thirty years ago were the old gray mastodons: the Sun Life building and Marie Reine du Monde. When he sat on the park bench the city fell away in bluffs and terraces down to the river. Cool air rose from the invisible water like a sea breeze, bringing the smell of fresh ironing.

Not the smell of ironing: the stench of it, the way all ripeness implies rancidness and rot. He could smell the stench of foul clothes right down to the sweat and sebum and the powders that lay against them. He could smell the scorch of cotton and, faintly, the odour of searing flesh.

Most children find the image of their parent's sexuality amusing if not ridiculous. Many children of older parents of his generation felt they were spawned in some awkward and accidental effort, never before attempted, never later duplicated. Porter had carried that feeling for many years.

But by the time he married and embarked on his own

tenuous course, he began seeing his parents in heroic and tragic dimensions: his mother a frail Giacometti; his father a squat, fierce Rodin. He saw his father as the existential beast, his mother as the balance of restraining forces, consumed by contraries. He carried that image of their heroic decimation into his adulthood and into his writing. And his writing to date had been of himself, the adolescent yo-yo, the little rubber ball restrained by his mother's frail rubber cord, whacked by his father's paddle.

It was two o'clock on a July morning in the last fifteen years of the twentieth century. A different generation in a different city in a country he no longer recognized had taken over. The only continuity between that winter morning at this spot and this summer night were the defunct buildings and the diseased synapses in Porter's brain.

14

She met him at the door of her apartment, dressed for summer in a wide straw hat and peasant skirt, Indian top and sandals. "I thought we could drive up north," she said, and she'd even packed a wicker basket with lunch and wine. They'd go to her mountain cabin near Ste-Agathe and spend the rest of the week in the cool air on a lake. In fact, she'd come back to town only for Corinne's party and to meet him. Friends had been using it; that's why he couldn't stay the night before.

Porter had walked over the mountain from Côte-des-

Neiges and Camilien-Houde to near Côte-Ste-Catherine where she lived. It was a muggy day climbing to the nineties; the mountains were appealing, and a lake would be nice, but nothing could match a quiet air-conditioned apartment on a sidestreet in Outremont.

"Do we have to go?" he asked. And he followed her silently back through the living-room into her bedroom where he lay on the bed and untied his shoes as she stood in front of the closet, slowly undoing her day's preparations. She laid the straw hat on a ledge, stepped out of the sandals and loosened the pearl earrings and placed them on the dresser. It was the slowest, most orderly undressing in Porter's long experience, as she took down the hangers, the hooks, for both their sets of clothes.

"Would you like to shower?" she asked, and yes, he said, he would. The serene lack of urgency was something new and unexpected, for last night, thinking of Madeleine Choquette as he lay awake in his tourist room, he'd all but phoned her at four in the morning, all but taken a taxi out and pounded on her door. Minutes later she slid the shower door open and stepped inside with him, and they stood wrapped together under the warm waterhead until it seemed to him that air and flesh and water were continuous and he had stepped out of his body altogether.

They were lying on the translator's bed, talking for the first time since last night. She'd been playing little translation games, confessing small confusions with English, even after twenty years of intimacy. "There's a sign on the Thruway going down to Albany," she said, " 'Trucks Under 40 Use Low Gear,' and my first impression was, *How very old their trucks are!* Or last winter, the TV weatherman in Plattsburgh said, 'Expect six quick inches of snow,' and I panicked! What's a 'quick inch'? Is that like a country mile? Even last night when you said you had to go straight back to New York, I first thought, well, I certainly hope he's not going to get *bent* first! You see what I mean? And then I hit sentences in your book like, 'I spun my mental Rolodex and her name came up . . .' How am I supposed to deal with that in French?''

He ran the palm of his hand up her body, resting it on her cheek, then back down. They had cooled off, returned to their separate bodies. ''Madeleine,'' he said, ''help me.''

She pressed cool fingertips to his eyes.

''I'm lost,'' he said.

''I'm here. I'm not going away.''

''I'm forty-six years old, Madeleine. By forty-six a man should have an ability to predict likely reactions. Utter ignorance should be pretty well eliminated. Total insecurity should be fairly unlikely . . . you know what I'm saying?''

''Those are American expectations. I'm fifty-two and my life is exactly the same. I don't know anyone's whose isn't.''

''My mother was fifty-two,'' he said.

''Don't think I don't know. I was almost afraid to mention it.''

''My epilepsy has come back.''

''I know. I saw it last night at dinner.''

''I don't know how to treat it. Last time, the medicine slowed me down. I couldn't take that again. I don't know if it's a medical condition or . . . a message, you know? My mind is falling apart. I haven't written in over a year.

I have a new family, but I don't feel like I belong to them . . . . I feel like a monster, sometimes."

He felt like a blind man, trying to assemble a thousand-piece jigsaw puzzle.

"You were a Quebec Catholic once," she said. "Remember the consolations of melancholy."

She lifted her fingers. She crouched over him, a full, immense woman of fifty years, her breasts whiter than milk, nearly touching his eyes. She was a smiling haze above him, grey hair without striking features. Then she buried her face in his, her lips on his, and the long, erotic nightmare of his life began to build. He was conscious of the presence of sin in what his body was doing, impurities linked to the dusty hallways of his childhood and adolescence and the dingy lights of de Bullion Street and none of it mattered. He would have handed over his soul at that moment for just twenty more minutes like this, fifteen, ten, and when it was over and they were lying still in one another's arms, he fell asleep believing that no condition, moral or medical, could have survived those last eruptions intact.

15

He had a very active profile, cutting in and jutting out, like an ingenious edge to a jigsaw puzzle piece. Ageing was just a process of thinning here and thickening there, getting shorter, or stretching out. His hands were comparatively huge — arthritic, Porter supposed — and his forearms bulged like Popeye's, but the neck was frail and the cheeks were sunken. Porter would not have recognized him, and no one would have placed him in the same century, on the same continent, with his daughter.

He limped now — again, the arthritis, Corinne had mentioned on the drive out — and he hadn't worked since Paulette died. He was on disability, which paid the beer and the rent on a second-floor flat in Ville d'Anjou. He wasn't yet fifty, but he'd lost out on things.

It was Madeleine who'd persuaded him: see your cousin. "I met him when I was translating your book. He's a little sad, but he sincerely wants to meet you again." Then she'd said, "You know what he told me? He said, 'Knowing Phillie gave meaning to my life.' How's that, eh?"

Whenever Corinne visited her father, the neighbourhood gathered. "Coco, Coco," people shouted, and lined the sidewalk hoping for a glimpse. There should be a documentary in this, Porter thought: the New Quebec, built on the bones of men like Dollard. With Corinne and Richard, Madeleine and Porter all out on the front gallery and with a case of beer at his feet, Dollard Carrier was the soul of volubility. He reminded Porter of an artificial-heart recipient, an affable soul utterly confused by all the attention. Now he was waving down to the passers-by, toasting them with a beer at eleven in the morning, giving his daughter loud kisses and keeping one enormous paw on Porter's knee.

"Some times we had, eh?" he laughed, rolling a cigarette. "Christ, this guy comes up from the States and steals my bed. Him and his parents, breezes into our little flat down in Hochelaga that was already jammed . . . goddamn, I hated him at first. Couldn't understand a word of English, of course. I must have made life hell for you, Phillie, I'm sorry. I never apologized. I'm not right sometimes. Stupid, that's what I am. No, no . . . you took it all like a man and surprised the shit out of me, I'll admit it. You were weak and twice as smart as anyone else, and I couldn't say it then but I'll say it now — I was damned proud of you."

Corinne winked at Porter; Madeleine squeezed his arm. Richard asked, "Did you hear him on Coco's show?"

"Naw, she knows about me. Can't understand her on the radio, speaks too high class for me to follow. Give me a baseball game or a hockey match."

"I was sorry to hear about Paulette," said Porter.

"She was a good woman," said Dollard, dipping his head. He held up a new beer; he was drinking alone.

"Dollard —" and now Porter moved closer and put his arm on his cousin's shoulder. "My mother, you remember, killed herself?"

Dollard crossed himself. "Terrible thing. A tragedy," he muttered.

"I wondered if anyone ever talked about it. One thing was, my father wanted a divorce. She was carrying the papers with her when she died."

"We don't believe in divorce," he said. "Everyone else is getting a divorce nowadays. Not me and Paulette. Twenty-three years married, praise her soul, six good kids. Already two of the boys — Coco's brothers, there — they got divorces. You understand what's happening, Phillie?"

"No, I don't." If he could have answered he might have said, twenty years of intimacy is too heavy a burden for the human heart. What he said was, "I was hoping for word of my father. You're the only person I can ask."

Until he'd come back to Montreal, Porter had felt comparatively young. Now he felt like the last of his generation, the last, along with Madeleine and maybe a few old priests and nuns, who remembered the bad, murderous and suicidal old days. It was a culture made for incongruities. Dollard and Corinne; Dollard and himself.

"Uncle Reggie," said Dollard. "My father always warned me about Uncle Reggie."

"What happened to him, Dollard?"

"He was a restless man, Phillie. That's what my father always said."

"Where is he?"

"It's a Home — St Justin's out in Laval. He's an old, old man. The sisters do what they can. Sometimes he must ask for me, and they come over and get me."

"What does he say, when he asks for you?"

"Nothing. He forgets, or probably he never asked. They have to keep busy, too. I don't mind."

"Does he ask about *me*? About his son?"

Dollard turned slowly and looked down at his beer. "He doesn't have a son, not where he is."

16

They were lying in bed after another day of not making it past the front hallway of Madeleine's apartment. She had greeted him now three days running, freshly showered and crisply dressed, as though ready for tennis or a long afternoon in a rented punt, a picnic from straw hampers in an Impressionist glade. But she would close the door and move to her well-stocked closet and casually begin undressing. She scattered the hangers on the bed, and they hung up their clothes in silence. And they would lie together as though they'd already been out, taken their exercise and now were back for rest.

She made him feel he was on perpetual vacation in some tropical resort, passing his mornings in strenous touring then stealing a few hours for drinks, sex and slumber while the rest of the tour was on a dusty bus visiting ruins. She was the oldest woman in his life; the only older woman in his life.

And then they would talk. About his parents, his childhood, her family, her children, his children; her adjustments to the States when her family had moved down there, his to Montreal; about her writing, his writing. Madeleine had left the States when her marriage failed ("Husbands can forgive their wives hating them, so long as they don't learn to love other men," she said), but she'd gone to Paris and lived there ten years, working in publicity. She was going to stay, thinking that Quebec held nothing for her. She started writing in Paris. Quebec writers and singers were just beginning to catch on in France, after three hundred years of ridicule.

Her children were Americans, they'd stayed back in Boston with their English-speaking father. And why did she leave Paris? Something so small, really, but one of those potent moments that forced her to examine her irrelevance in France. "A perforation in the fabric of indifference," she called it.

"I was walking with my lover in the Bois de Vincennes,

passing to the Parc Floral.'' She named those places as though Porter had seen them, as though any cultured person knew them intimately. "We had to take a subterranean passage under a stone bridge. There were unpleasant piss-odours, but that's not uncommon on the streets of Paris. No, it was the graffiti sprayed on the walls of the passage: *Mort aux juifs*, and *Violer les filles arabes* and *Purité aryenne*, and dozens of condoms, hundreds of them, slippery underfoot. My friend was roaring with laughter — he'd *brought* me there deliberately! It was all *funny* to him, you see. He was a very sophisticated, socialist lawyer, but he said he liked to come down there to 'get in touch with his feelings.'

"The obscenities weren't on the walls — they were in his politics, and I'd never appreciated that before. When I got upset he called me a typical reactionary Quebec cow. To him, the problem was I couldn't take a good joke.''

Porter had had no such moments, at least, none that he remembered. He envied people their moments of clear hate, knowing their own names and where they were born, their small perforations. He hungered for clear distinctions. What this visit had awakened in him was the realization of his fundamental Quebec Catholicism, the Jansenist belief that there is no end to the implications of a single act.

One day in Pittsburgh when he was twelve years old and living in utter harmony even with his epilepsy, his father went to work and learned he'd been fired without warning. "My name was Phil Porter, my father was Reg Porter and we were Americans from Pittsburgh.

"Then in one moment my father hauls off and slugs the man sitting at his desk and runs from the store. I wake up the next morning without the parents I thought I knew, without the name I thought I had, without a city or a country or even a language I could speak! And because of that I become split down the middle, my mother kills herself and I'm sitting here in middle age and I'm still running."

Madeleine ran her fingers over his shoulder, down his arm and flank. "Why do you think you're epileptic?" she asked.

"I was battered by a baby-sitter's husband when I was three, in Cincinnati."

"I know that's what you wrote."

He gathered her fingers in a stunted bunch of carmine nails. "Wasn't I?"

"Isn't it time to find out?"

"I don't remember any of it. The earliest memory I have is of sitting in the kitchen sink and being bathed. I remember Johnny Mercer singing 'Don't Fence Me In' on the radio, and I sang along with him. And I remember sitting next to my father on the arm of his chair, and I fell off and broke my arm."

"I'll tell you what I think, Philip. You're the one who's always so amazed by *mutations*, right? You keep looking at Coco and saying, 'How did it happen?' like she's some kind of miracle. And you look at Dollard like he's a caveman or something —"

"A fish," said Porter. "I'm a mud-puppy."

"Okay, whatever. But Philip, there's no such thing as a mutation here. Where's the transition between *your* father and *you*? It's your mother, right? and between Dollard and Coco — it's *you*, that's who. *We're* the transition, Coco's a transition, your little daughter who plays

Chopin and Mozart, *she's* a transition. There aren't any permanent forms of *anything*, Porter darling. Where did you pick up that museum mentality? Listening to you is like going on a tour of Ste Anne de Beaupré or Lourdes or Brother André's Shrine — it's medieval! You look at life like it's some kind of before-and-after picture. Either it's totally damned or it's too good to include you. That's old Quebec Catholicism, darling. You're holding out for a miracle to come down and save you."

17

There are no permanent forms, except perhaps the styles of institutional Catholic architecture: schools, hospitals, convents, nursing homes. The muggy weather had begun to break when Porter made his way alone over the back river to the island of Laval. Maison St-Justin could be spotted from half a mile away, a battlement of yellow brick in the middle of unvarying fieldstone duplexes.

Grey Sisters ran the place; they made Porter nervous. St Justin's seemed to be in a permanent state of renovation, like Olympic Stadium with its cranes, the result of insufficient public money beginning to supplant the church. Ladders and scaffolding, dropcloths, uncured dry-wall and brightly painted television rooms were jammed into dingy, cream-coloured corridors with varnished oak doors, set with stippled glass. The number of Greys thinned out on the upper floors; rough-looking orderlies with lips curled cruelly over hockey scars seemed to be in control. His father was listed on the fourth floor. Dozens of old men in striped hospital pyjamas lined the halls in wheelchairs. The opened doors of the wards showed only withered legs and bony toes pointing up at silent television screens.

He asked one of the orderlies for M'sieur Carrier's room. The young man snickered, but gave out a number. "Reggie," he winked. "*Reggie, l'américain!*"

And then there was no delaying it. He stood at the base of his father's bed staring the length of his father's body, from the bare feet up the shins and over the sleeping chest to the enormous nostrils, the flaring eyebrows, and the immense pink ears, caught by the pillow and spread out full. His mouth was open as he snored. The teeth were out; his father had become all cavities, air was claiming him.

Over the bed hung a crucifix.

He took a chair at the head of the bed. The plastic wristband around the bundle of purple veins read "Carrier, R." He remembered his father as a snorer and heavy sleeper. He held his father's hand and gave it a firm tug.

"Dad?"

The eyes were open. Porter thought he read panic. He cranked up the bed. His father didn't seem strong enough to sit up straight. "Dad, it's me, Philip."

No recognition. He wanted his teeth; his eyes told him that. He slipped them in without any problems, then cleared his throat. This was as long as his father had normally gone without a cigarette. Such a drastic change as that — what had it cost him? When had he done it? Who had suffered through it with him?

The male orderly came to the door, accompanied by a nun. "M'sieur Carrier," she said, "there's much to talk about."

Fees? he wondered. He couldn't afford his father's care; didn't feel he owed it.

His father cleared his throat, smiled briefly, and fluttered his hand in the nun's direction.

"Sometimes we can't shut him up." She repeated it louder, for his father's benefit. "Eh, Reggie? He looks confused right now."

"I thought, all these years . . . " Porter began, "he was lost. Gone. Totally out of my life."

He felt his French deserting him. Fear of the nun, back to the time when he was learning the language under the unforgiving tutelage of Soeur Timothée. She'd had a nickname; that too had deserted him. He realized he had never spoken French to his father, despite the fact that his father's Frenchness had helped destroy his life.

"He did not list you among his immediate family."

"That is nevertheless my father," said Porter. If this was a Catholic home, he didn't want to jeopardize his father's care by too much disclosure. "My mother has been dead nearly thirty years. I went to the States and changed my name."

"That's your business, of course. If all the papers are in order, we can release him to you," she said.

"I can't look after him."

"So you came here for what? Curiosity? Will you sign papers attesting to your refusal, then? It is required, now that he is a ward of the province."

Porter signed. Bless socialized medicine; forms, not bills. He used his proper name, Philippe Carrier, *fils*.

"Dad? Do you know who I am?"

"This is your son, Reggie," she echoed, louder. She glanced down at his signature. "Philippe."

"He knew me as Phil. We always talked in English, so maybe, if you don't mind . . . . Dad, I haven't seen you in thirty years. I want to talk to you. I want to find out what you've been doing, where you've been . . . . Do you understand me?"

There were flickers in his eyes, as though he might have understood and then immediately suppressed it.

The orderly had worked his way to the head of the bed where he was untying the bow of the old man's gown and slipping it over his head. His father slumped forward a little, and the orderly took out the pillow.

His father was obviously starving to death. What kind of man lets his father starve to death? Porter wondered. He probably weighed well under a hundred pounds, and the dead white skin was marked with bruises, nicks, veins and scars that Porter had never seen.

He must bruise like a peach, he thought.

"You might help us here, Mr Carrier," said the nun. "We try to account for as much of the medical history of the patient as seems relevant. Your father has had quite an extensive medical involvement." She traced the still-red scars of abdominal surgery, indicated more whorls of stitching in his groin — "Hernia, we had to do that" — and then tipped him forward to show deep, smooth scars under the shoulder blades. "A lucky man — lung-cancer operation, at least ten years old. We have a fairly complete record from your brother in Ottawa, but he couldn't tell us —"

"— my brother?"

"Yes, of course. He often visits, along with your sisters. They're much better than you've been, you'll forgive my commenting. Technically, your father should be moved to a more medically oriented facility — this is still for the ambulatory and continent, and you can see your father is not in that category."

"I'll sign," he said.

"And one more thing, just for our legal records. There's this scar on his back —" she tipped him forward like a slab of meat into Porter's arms and loosened the knot of his clean gown. "What do you know of this?"

He had never noticed a scar; to him, his father was unblemished. His parents had never undressed in front of him, except for his mother that one time. And now, today. His father after thirty years smelled the same, the same powders, the same sweat, the same ştale cotton odours, but with age the ripeness had turned putrid. My God, don't they bathe him here? Should *I* bathe him? He pulled his father closer, loosening the robe that melted from his dead-white shoulders. It was like baby's flesh rubbed in flour, red at the slightest touch, scabs clustered where his collar bone had nearly poked through. He knew even before he saw it what he would find.

It was an old, discoloured patch of skin, shaped like a shark's fin, a neat, purple parabola. It wasn't deep, but it was extensive, and it had withstood the shrinking of his body and the loosening of his skin. It looked like a decal ready to be pulled off.

"I don't think it gives him pain," the nun said, "but watch —"

She touched it with her ballpoint pen, and Porter's father lunged forward, hard against his chest. "You see, there's sensitivity there — or maybe a memory of it, locked away. You could stick pins in the rest of his skin and he wouldn't feel them. His circulation is entirely gone — he can't move his feet, and they're like chunks of ice to the touch."

"Don't you operate?"

"We must justify the expense, m'sieur. Your father is not likely to survive surgery — or live long enough to benefit from it."

He could feel his father's breathing, his heart pounded fast as a bird's against his arm. He stared down his father's back at the patch of discoloured skin rising like a shark's pointed snout breaking water, and he felt a twist of terror.

"I think I know," he said. "It's shaped like an iron, isn't it?"

"What kind of man brands himself with an iron on his own backside? Your brother said he'd always had it."

"A man like my father," said Porter. "A woman like my mother." Then, savouring the words, "My brother was always a particularly unobservant boy."

He laid his father down, straightening the new gown and centring his head on the pillow. He could smell the ironed clothes, deep in his brain. "My father remembers the iron, I'm sure, don't you?" He showed signs of wanting to speak, but again held back. Porter stifled an urge to ask for an iron and bring it close, and closer, to his father's face. Deep in the brain, the intruder ran from room to room, and Porter turned on the lights, chased, blocked the escape routes.

"That scar happened over forty years ago, when I was three years old. My mother was ironing clothes. My father was bathing me in the kitchen sink. And I started screaming. Why, I don't know." But he remembered it vividly: the record playing "Don't Fence Me In," the water, and being lifted and dropped, lifted and dropped, and his head striking the porcelain partition between the sinks. "I didn't remember it till this minute."

The nun seemed not to notice.

He turned to her. "Get me a sponge and some water, please."

He gathered his father's head in his arms and pressed his lips on his forehead, his cheeks and then his lips. He stared into the grey eyes that gave nothing back, praying for just another sign of recognition, and then his father closed his eyes.

"Sleep, father," he said. "I have loved you all my life."

18

They met him in Poughkeepsie station and drove him home. He'd been gone just under a week, but they had news! Hannah had learned a new sonata that she wanted to play for Poppy that very night, tired or not.

"Have you learned some things, too?" Petra asked him as they cleaned the dishes later that evening.

"I'll see the doctor in the morning. He said he can dose me, so I'll let him try."

"You didn't really believe in miracle cures, did you?"

"I'm afraid I did." He took her into his arms. "I've

learned many wonderful things from many wonderful people, but I did not learn any miracle cure for epilepsy."

She didn't struggle, as she often did. She even returned the hug and lingered for a kiss. "We've missed you. Well, Hannah's been too busy to really *miss* you, but I've missed you."

When the dishes were dry, they moved to the livingroom and sat quietly as their daughter began to play.

Autobiographical Fragment: Memories of Unhousement

Memories of Unhousement

Memories of Unhousement

I was born in Fargo, North Dakota, in 1940. Along with Roger Maris and William Gass and Larry Woiwode. In that *Ragtime* spirit that haunts us all, I sometimes think of my mother pushing the pram, of Mrs. Woiwode pushing hers, of little Roger Maris, then six, dashing past us, bat on shoulder. Billy Gass, a bifocular teenager, squints a moment at these figures of life, then returns to the ice castle of his imagination, "The Pedersen Kid" crystallizing even then. *Beyond the Bedroom Wall* gurgles in his stroller. Babe Ruth's assassin takes a few mean cuts.

I am the only Canadian writer born in Fargo, North Dakota.

There is nothing obscure, really, about Fargo. In 1977, at a cocktail party in New Delhi, India, where my India-born wife, Bharati, was serving that year as a quasi-diplomat for a Canadian educational exchange, I found myself talking to an agreeable, white-haired American with a professorial manner, the U.S. agricultural attaché. I was merely a spouse, conscious of a peripheral role.

"I consider myself half a Canadian, really," he said.

"I'm more than half American myself," I replied. What it is that I am, fundamentally, is a matter of earnest agony to me. We shared a smile, wondering which of us would be the first to break. One-time Canadians in America have no problem; erstwhile Americans in Canada will always feel a little guilty. "I was born in North Dakota," I confessed. Then, covering my tracks, "My parents had just come down from Winnipeg."

"I was about to say the same thing. Where in North Dakota?"

"Fargo."

"Amazing."

He was the first North Dakotan I had ever met. "What year would that have been," he asked. "Forty, forty-one?"

"April 1940."

"I was just finishing my M.A. at North Dakota State that spring. My wife was an O.B. nurse."

Parallel lives were beginning to converge, as though a collision course plotted by children on separate planets had suddenly become inevitable. We said together, "St John's Hospital?"

I added, "Dr Hanna?"

He called his wife over. As she put her drink down and turned to join us, he said, "How would you like to meet the person who delivered you?"

Before the Interstate system obliterated the old America, you used to come across them at country crossroads:

clusters of white arrows tipped in black, pointing in every direction. Somewhere on the plains you would see it, stop, and be thrilled: DENVER 885, it would say, or NEW ORLEANS 1045 or, better yet, LOS ANGELES 2000. Who decided on the city and the mileage, I'll never know. Perhaps they had taken over from the whitewashed rocks, the dabs of tar left by earlier waves of impatient travellers, when twenty or thirty miles a day was more than fair measure. Nowadays, the green mirror-studded billboards conspire to keep our minds on the effortlessly attainable, the inevitable. No more than two destinations, they seem to say; don't tease us with prospects greater than our immediate ambition.

We are deprived of that special thrill when our destination, our crazy, private destination, made its first appearance in one of those black-tipped clusters. No reason at all that on a road between Chicago and Madison, just outside Beloit, Wisconsin, WINNIPEG should miraculously appear. Yet in 1949 when I was nine and guiding my father on our longest trip home, it did. Nine hundred miles in a '47 Chevy with its split windshield, high fenders and curved chrome bars over the dashboard radio was a typical fifteen-hour long haul for my salesman-father.

How, I think now, he must have wanted to delay it. He, who delayed nothing in his life, a man lacking all patience. For old times' sake, he said, we'd spend the night in Detroit Lakes, Minnesota. That's where they'd honeymooned. Up there in the headwaters of the Mississippi is where I was conceived.

We always returned to Winnipeg whenever my father ran out of work, or was run out of work, or town. We had left Fargo in 1941, Cincinnati in '43, Pittsburgh in '45 and — a week before — Leesburg, Florida. Every time we left, we headed back to Winnipeg, my mother's city.

My father was from the village of Lac Mégantic, a few mountain ridges north of Maine, directly south of Quebec City. Winnipeg must have been a torture to him. I remember him, slicing luncheon meats in an upstairs bedroom next to a leaking window in my grandmother's house, sipping forbidden beer and smoking Canadian cigarettes — their aroma so much nuttier than his American Tareytons — though Canadian corktips inflamed his lips.

He never spoke of his dislikes, he merely acted on them, without warning. He was probably not entirely sane.

My father possessed — or rather, it possessed him — a murderous temper. He had pounded out twenty victories in three weight divisions in two countries under various names that served him like flags of convenience, before getting knocked out — and quitting, he said, though my mother came to doubt it, years later — by Bat Battalino, an eventual champion. The kindest interpretation my mother could put on his behaviour in later life was brain damage: "All that pounding he took." To this day, I love boxing, and I realize that somewhere around the radios and under the porch lights of my childhood in two dozen cities, I absorbed the pointers of boxing. My father's friends, if it could be said he had friends and not just cronies, had often been boxers. The violence of boxing, of his language, of his friends, of American life in general, drove my mother indoors.

Boxing credentials were good for one thing in Montreal in the 1920s. The career path took him to Canada's most successful export industry, helping assure, through bribery and intimidation, the delivery of Montreal's finest whisky to Prohibition-dry New York.

The first return to Canada that I remember was 1945, following an assault charge against my father in Pittsburgh. We crossed into Canada that midnight at Niagara Falls and were in Winnipeg three days later. Canada was still at war, the same war (I'm told) that had sent us to North Dakota six years earlier. Canada, part of Britain's war effort, would be on the front lines, everyone thought, as soon as the Luftwaffe finished mopping up. Lindbergh assured us it wouldn't take long. German U-Boats already controlled the Gulf of St Lawrence. The French-owned islands of St Pierre and Miquelon, off the coast of the British colony of Newfoundland, were rebelling against the Vichy régime; no one knew how long that would last, a fog-bound Casablanca. Once Britain fell, Newfoundland and Labrador would of course be ceded to the Nazis, just like the Channel Islands. The Frenchies in Quebec refused to fight an English war anyway; Adrien Arcand and his Brownshirts were poised for a coup whenever Hitler ordered it. All of which had left Ontario, in 1939 and '40, feeling itself in the probable front line of combat. Even the *bunds* of Buffalo and Detroit were stirring up border hate. The Ottawa River would become America's Marne. And so my parents had fled. I would be born in isolationist, accommodationist America. My father could be whatever he wanted to be, not just a dirty Frog in English Canada.

This is my first memory of Canada: the soldiers at Canadian customs, their jaunty berets. The smell of a different tobacco in the air. My Winnipeg uncle in his colonel's rough khaki, deep lines and dark skin, bushy eyebrows and salt-and-pepper hair, his thick moustache and his short, stocky body, reminding me years later of a Sandhurst-trained Israeli. One summer morning when I was five he had taken me and my cousins out on the lawn — he in his full uniform, the rows of First World War medals on his chest — and smoked glass for us. The scientists of the Free World had gathered in Winnipeg in 1945 for a spectacular view of a solar eclipse. I remember my twin cousins, limber girls of eight, doing backward flips all around my grandmother's house.

My first long exposure to Canada took place five years later, following one of my father's failures in central Florida. We'd driven up from Leesburg, those clustered signposts serving us well: ATLANTA 600, CHICAGO 1000. Yankee place-names frightened me; I was a southerner, I drawled inexcusably (I was soon to learn, in Winnipeg schools), I was as ignorant as a mudfish of history and mathematics. Yet travel excited me; in the bullet of a bus, the cab of a car, the world is concentrated, all perspectives converge. We tore around America, rolling double sixes on that old Monopoly board of two-lane blacktop. One day for Florida, another for the pine flats of Georgia. Then they came fast: Tennessee, Kentucky, Indiana, Illinois and, before the half-week was out, that sign in Beloit: WINNIPEG 945. We were in the green and watery states now, the Land o' Lakes and Sky Blue Waters in the lee of Canada — I expected moose, bear. We were in Fargo for an afternoon, and I wandered down the main street of my absurdly obscure hometown. We drove past the house we'd lived in that spring of 1940: Fifth Street S.E. My mother pointed out where the Hinckles had lived, the man who took all my baby pictures.

Many years later, when my first book of stories was published, I got a letter from a nursing home in Minneapolis. Mrs Hinckle had read the review in the *Star*. There couldn't be two Clark Blaises, not born in Fargo of Canadian parents, she said. I had to be the sweetest little baby she'd ever seen, the one my mother had worried over, the one her late husband had adored.

How like my mother, I think now, to have found another woman, in Fargo, who would remember names, who would read books and reviews, even in a nursing home. My mother's friends; my father's friends.

Of all the distinctions I have invented in my life and come to believe in with the force of myth, the difference between Canada and the United States — so frail in reality, so inconsequential in the consciousness of America or the world or even most Canadians — is still my last, my most important illusion. It matters to me, or it mattered until very recently, that a border exists. That people so similar should be formed in such different ways. That because I inherited those differences, I should have something special to say on both sides of the border.

I was *invaded* by geography the way other self-conscious youngsters are invaded by God, by music, by poetry, or a butterfly's wing. Through my childhood and adolescence and well into my adulthood and the ragged fringes of middle age, the faith in a Canada being of a different order of history, experience and humanity granted me an identity. It was never easy to claim it, but I never doubted it was there and that I belonged to it. Canada was always the large, locked attic of my sensibility, something I would never *know*, but was obliged to invent; it cultivated a part of me that America never touched. The significant blob of otherness in my life has always been Canada; it sits like a helmet over the United States, but I seemed to be the only person who felt its weight.

North, North, North: that glorious direction, and the provincial bison shield of Manitoba, the narrow highway that cut through the wheat fields to the west and the French-speaking hamlets along the Red River to the east, their lone church steeples gleaming (to my mother's disgust) higher than the bluffs that hid the rest of the town, rising even taller than the wheat elevators that stretched westward, each of them announcing a calloused, sun-reddened Protestant or Ukrainian town. And then, the highway divided, trolley tracks appeared and we were in Winnipeg.

I think often of the compass points. Like the arrow clusters at cramped country crossroads, the cardinal directions still move me; I dream restlessly of the eternal *setting out*, steering on to a highway for what I know will be a long drive and reading that first, firm challenge to the continent. *East*. And I see fishing boats and a pounding Winslow Homer rocky surf and the great cities, and I think, *yes*, that's the direction for me. Culture, history, people, excitement, sophistication. But then, on my drives to the Pacific, I thrill to those days of unbroken signposts, the barren miles of low hills and bluffs and promotional museums of forgivable, fake-historical tackiness, and I think, *West, West*, let me ride to the ridge, let me be free. Well, this time it was *North*: this was just about as far north as anyone from Florida could think of going. This was the western end of the Canadian Shield; east of here and the town names turn French and the faces along the highway are unmistakably Indian. West of here, golden fields of the world's hardest wheat.

I know the South — *South* — too well. It's the only compass point that fails to conjure a dreamlike essence. When I think of the Florida I knew, I remember only walls of leggy pine with slash marks on their trunks, hung with resin buckets, and I remember the Coke machines in country gas stations where for a nickel I could lift a heavy metal lid (I can remember the first whiff of that cold, moist air; I remember the pleasure of trailing my fingers in the dark, iced water), of spotting a bottle cap in one of the metal tracks and gliding it along to the spring catch my nickel had released. And I can remember draining those stubby little Coke bottles with their raised, roughened letters on the side, always checking the bottom to see where it had been bottled, how far it had come, though nearly all were good ol' bottles from Plant City and Orlando. Well, all I remember of *South* is sand and heat and thirst and skies the colour of sweaty undershirts. I remember the years of childhood, alternating threat with nightmare.

On Wolseley Avenue in Winnipeg, on the banks of the Assiniboine, my grandparents had their house. Three houses away, my aunt and uncle had an even larger home, with a garage full of canoes and kayaks and a basement full of hunting rifles and decoys and a special room for a billiards table. Since my uncle was in those days a writer and commercial artist as well as president of the Wheat Pool and Ducks Unlimited — and was soon to become Winnipeg's best-known television personality — and my aunt was a broadcaster, they had studios and libraries on the second floor. The third floor held guest rooms and an attic full of bundled magazines going back to the beginnings of *National Geographic* and *Reader's Digest*, as well as the splashy American weeklies like *Life* and *Collier's* and *The Saturday Evening Post*. They kept the hunting and fishing magazines and everything Canadian, particularly everything relating to the prairies and especially the Assiniboia region of Manitoba. My uncle (still alive and now in his nineties) had been a Homesteader, one of Manitoba's founders. Nothing important had ever been thrown out. The house was virtually a computer, although means of retrieval were still a little primitive.

That house, and their lives, represented something to me called Canada, that was more than merely attractive; it was compelling. In the various towns of my first ten years, we had always lived in small apartments carved out of old servants' quarters, on the fringes of other people's families, and we always seemed to be sharing some vital function of other peoples' lives. Kitchens, bathrooms, entrances, hallways, washing facilities and later, when we moved back to the States in the early fifties, televisions. Whatever the reasons, Canada, by virtue of its cool, English houses and its politeness and its streetcars and its formalities and its formidable understanding of the world outside — as brought to us every day by the BBC noon news — was a more comprehensible and interesting place to live than America. Not that America was ever excluded. It's just that Canadians, like long-suffering spouses, knew they would be forced to know everything about America, while America knew nothing, cared nothing, for them.

My parents had moved back to Canada at a time when its differences from the United States were unforced but unequivocal. Canada was like a heavy novel that others found dull and difficult but that I found accessible from the beginning, thanks to my accidental placement inside an emblematically Canadian family. I visited my aunt and uncle every day and shot pool in the basement by myself or with my cousin. My parents and I were staying in the second-floor bedroom and study at my grandmother's. Between the houses and school, I became a Canadian.

My grandmother was a classic of the grandmother type; too old to have a life of her own, but young enough to manage the lives of several others. She was small but sturdy, she had wit and a deadpan delivery that could "really get me going" as she put it. She had taken up driving and a wee bit of smoking and brandy drinking (the sign of an amateur in these matters; she kept her cigarettes loose in an old sugar bowl in the kitchen cupboard), and she would smoke only at predictable times in the morning and evening, when the dough was rising after a good punch-down.

My grandfather, when awake, was the focus of our awareness, though not of our attention. While he was up, we all kept an eye on him. He was classically senile; a bald, tall, stooped old patriarch, a one-time doctor, a breeder of flowers and fruit trees and an importer of draft horses, the consolidator of an insurance group, now the largest in Canada — a man of great substance in western Canada. Up on the second floor, in the room occupied by my parents and me, I would read the volumes of *Who's Who in Western Canada* that told my grandfather's tale ("The Luther Burbank of Canada" with the names of his prize-winning Clydesdales), and I never tired of reading the biographies of him in the Canadian *Reader's Digest*, and all the profiles in the medical and insurance journals. I learned to feel a touch of family pride whenever we passed an office of the Wawanesa Mutual, the insurance company he'd built. *Everyone* in Winnipeg seemed to be rich and famous and confident; all of my relatives had power and recognition; casual visitors to my uncle and aunt's house turned out to be cabinet ministers, American governors, authors. When I walked down the street with my aunt or uncle, people stopped and often turned around to watch us. After the bruised, violent, anonymous lives we'd lived in those mildewed southern towns, Winnipeg was a jolt of pure, cold oxygen, the only place left in the world that conformed to the notions of reality, and of a happy childhood, that I'd gotten from reading, or my own intense imagining.

At the age of seventy-five, my grandfather was merely a disturbing presence. He was strong and stern, and he kept himself busy through a ten-hour workday in his old study and sometimes in the living-room, underlining every sentence in every book and magazine in the house. He did not know his name, or that of his wife and daughters (he'd had nine daughters and one son, and all five of the survivors visited regularly, except the son in Toronto and my mother, the eldest). His memory had deserted him rapidly while he was still in his sixties, and as a doctor he'd recognized it — it had been his father's fate as well — and had gotten out of medicine and cut back on the insurance. He'd retired, physically exhausted after paying back hundreds of thousands of dollars of Depression debts (always explained to me as the failure of American farmers to pay him for the Clydesdales he'd imported), but the insurance company had treated him generously. His faculties continued to fail. He was apparently alert enough in 1940, however, when my mother brought me up from Fargo for my first visit, to feel the bumps on my head and declare, "Don't worry, Annie, this boy will never be a fighter." So far as I can determine, he never spoke to me, or of me, again. His heart repaired itself under the protective seal of a worry-free dementia, and he still had his work, the underlining of every word in the daily *Free Press*, and all those stacks of magazines upstairs. That was my Canada, and that was my grandfather's house; a place where everything was intact and even madness could be quietly accommodated. There was, in fact, only one thing that could not be housed, because he was not organically a part of it, and that was my father.

"See what *he* wants," my grandmother would ask, not unkindly. She was as afraid of giving offence as my father was; therefore they worked out elaborate systems of mutual avoidance. He rarely came downstairs. When he did, an aroma of tobacco preceded him by at least half a minute, and my grandfather would lay his pencil down, carefully marking his place in the work still before him, stand, and — high, quivering voice fierce with outrage — order him out. "How dare you, sir, walk across my carpet with your dirty boots? Out, out, I say!" My father, in Winnipeg, never went outside in the winter, and was always in slippers. My grandfather was furious, muttering, "The cheek, the gall! I will report this, don't think I won't!" That would be a sign for my mother, first, to interpose herself. "It's all right, Daddy, he's Leo, your son-in-law." Now my grandfather was in a proper Victorian rage — what was this middle-aged woman *doing* in his house, insulting him with familiar names and sluttish behaviour? He threw my mother aside. "I don't know why you're shielding him, Lillie, but I'm getting to the bottom of this. I won't rest —" by which time my father had sneaked back up the stairs, cursing to himself, and my grandfather would be left standing, hands clenched, undecided over the next challenge, having already forgotten the source of the rage, remembering only that he was enraged and had to act it. All the women in his life now were "Lillie," my grandmother's name, except my grandmother, who was usually just "mother." After he died, at the age of eighty-two, my grandmother had her own few bad years, heaping invectives on her husband, not for those last twenty inglorious years, but for the years of his magnificent achievement, the *Who's Who* years. Who or what to believe? Even as I write this, my own mother is enacting the dramas of her parents, and as I reach back into these events of thirty or more years ago, I'm aware that truth is simply a matter of framing and reframing. I've chosen to believe certain versions; I've rejected others. I too was blessed with a gifted memory, and I've worn it down by now to something dull and ordinary, and I write this in the terror that the family disease awaits me.

When my grandfather's fists unclenched, he'd go back to the chair and begin the assault on a new column of print.

The winter of 1949-50 was one of the snowiest in Winnipeg history. It would lead to a spring flood that is still remembered, to sandbags in my aunt's and grandmother's backyards, to those canoes and kayaks pushing off directly from the driveway and bringing relief a few blocks downstream. And, as the head of the Red Cross, it would be my aunt's finest hour: in the pictures we were sent (by that time we too had pushed off; they caught up with us in Cleveland, in a rooming house on Euclid Avenue), my aunt and uncle would be bundled in their parkas against the slanting sleet, under helmets with the red cross painted on the sides, and it would remind me of British air-raid wardens. The pictures were grainy, black and white, some of them smeared from rainwater on the lenses (a beautiful, accidental effect; what would be its equivalent in language?), as millions of dollars of property and boulders of ice, houses, and trucks hurtled past their houses, borne on the fury of a horizontal Niagara.

That would be the spring. Right now, it is still a hard, Siberian winter day. Winnipeg should not exist, except as an urban planner's act of defiance, an experiment on the heartless Russian model. Yet it does exist, like Edmonton exists, like Montreal exists, and the effects of that anomaly — the intense communalism, the isolation, the pride, the shame and absurdity of carrying on normal life at forty below zero — create a population of stubborn, sceptical survivalists, hungry for recognition and certification, a people born with the ache of anonymity and the conviction that they'll always have something to prove. All of which leads to that bone-proud prairie loneliness, the suspicion of anyone who's had it easier — east, west, or south. In my mother's family, self-reliance was a creed; bottled-up and bitten-back, no grief was exposed, no help asked for, though none was refused. There seemed to be a fear of softness, a numb acceptance of fate, a determination bordering on mission to make do with the cards that were dealt, to curse no one but oneself, and then only silently, or after sanity departed.

In my mother's family they constantly headed deeper north, as though to test themselves, as though Winnipeg itself were not test enough. My cousins began their kayaking at ten or so, portaging between rivers and lakes right to the shores of Hudson Bay. They had a farm a few miles west where they grew flax and ran trap lines, and in the fall I went with them — Florida child that I was, accent and all — and learned to shoot at an early enough age to avoid the usual reservations of an urban academic.

I have seen most of the northern hemisphere's major cities by now, but Portage Avenue in the early fifties remains for me something special, like a Russian movie, molded on a scale of epic tedium that nevertheless achieves a certain impressive weight. If we could rid our minds of notions of charm and beauty and still be receptive to urban grandeur, then Portage Avenue, the east-west axis of Winnipeg and half the province of Manitoba would stand as a model. It was conceived on a scale of spaciousness in keeping with the open fields and possibly in revenge for the two thousand miles of crabbed forest at its back. It was wide, straight and flat, and down its middle in its own *maidan* rolled the endless herd of rumbling streetcars. Standing at our corner, Stiles and Portage, I could look a couple of miles to the west, the buildings showing not a single variation in height and not a single uniformity of design, and spot, in embryo as it were, the line of streetcars that would be passing me in the next half hour. Since no one could stand outside for more than ten minutes anyway, it was most compassionate of the transport commission to flood the rails with more cars than any city had a right to expect. That was my Winnipeg; a city of prompt and endless convenience.

Up on the second floor in the bedroom we had converted to a small apartment, with a hotplate for my father's coffee and a small skillet for my mother's eggs — the smoke-filled haven of my father — a small drama was being enacted that would alter all our lives. My mother had reactivated her old teacher's permit and was, by now, substituting on a near-daily basis in various parts of the city. I was in school, struggling to overcome the deficiencies of a rural southern background. Thanks to family connections, I was not routinely demoted two grades, as were other American transfers, and was managing, with after-school tutoring, to make a successful transition to the world of ink and nibs, formulae and long compositions. I was singing British folk songs instead of the U.S. Military Academy Hymns. No one sang "God Save the King" or "O Canada" louder than I every morning in the hall. And for the first time, I was enjoying my classmates. In Florida, students were to be tolerated or avoided while pursuing the fugitive pleasures of the text. Here, there was no schoolyard fighting, despite the tempting foreign target I must have offered. The captains of the various team sports — most of them imposing Icelandic boys with names like Thorlaksen — would often choose me first, simply because I was American. They took the time to teach me the unfamiliar games, British Bulldog and broom hockey, and would even stop the action if they saw I was too hopelessly out of place. When ice hockey started, I was permitted to sit inside.

No one could have been more displaced than my father. He'd ask me when it was safe to go downstairs and to slip outside (this necessitated checking on my grandfather and enduring his scolding for having sneaked into the house "from the stables" and for having walked on the rugs). My father, Leo Romeo Blais, had been going across the river to French St Boniface and to the furniture stores of the *borax* North End, the parts of town rich in contacts for the salesman's life he knew. Like my mother, he had a transferable skill. He worked a few days and decided things were too slow, too old-fashioned. He didn't know the Canadian furniture scene any more, and the American brands, when carried, were far too expensive. Of course he didn't mention anything to us about working or where the search was taking him. That wouldn't be his style.

One day after school I went upstairs to read old magazines and the *Who's Who*. I had a phenomenal memory (the incarnation of my grandfather, according to the family); I was committing those rows of fine print to memory. My father was there at his place by the window, looking out on the snowy roof, up Stiles Street to Portage, in the distance. On his knees was a letter. On the window ledge were some notebook pages he must have taken from me. When he saw me, he folded the letter back in the envelope. I tried to show I wasn't interested, but a small suitcase on the bed was packed.

I went over to my cousin's to shoot pool. My grandfather was sleeping; my father would have no trouble sneaking out. I couldn't imagine where we'd be going next, but *West*, I remember, excited me. I felt ready for it now; it was the only direction we hadn't explored.

I played pool till the phone rang. My aunt called me from the head of the stairs. "Clark, your mother."

No, I said, I hadn't seen him. I didn't know anything about it. She was crying. What can I tell them? my mother wanted to know. She'd been downtown, looking for our own apartment. We were going to stay in Winnipeg, that had been the plan. *We'd agreed; we'd try to settle down. For Clark's sake.*

He was gone, all right. Shirts, suits, shoes and car; the salesman's clearing out. My mother was already reframing it for her mother and sisters: "Leo decided he could do better in the States. He's following a lead in . . . (I made it up, blocking out all alternatives) . . . Denver. He'll send for us when he finds an apartment." I even believed in Denver; I looked up a city map and tried to memorize the grid. Years later, pursuing my own studies of another Franco-American whose life — given a different dominance in our family, I might have crossed — I again encountered those heroic late-forties, and nineteen-fifty Denver streets of Neal Cassady and Jack Kerouac; madness to push this further, though a message to me seems to linger. Kerouac and Cassady were my father's world, the one he never escaped, of booze and fights and women and endless travel, and he died back inside it, buried in a plot of New Hampshire called "*le petit coin du Canada*," as desolately as Kerouac did in his mother's transplanted Lowell kitchen in Florida. Jack's father's name was also Leo.

On the sheet of notebook paper I found drafts of a letter. It said more or less what we expected: he'd gotten a lead, it looked good, and he always did better if he could interview in person. If he got it, we'd live better than we ever had. My mother, too, gazed out over the roof, up Stiles, at that one. No need to say the obvious.

She didn't care about the rest of the paper, which wasn't a proper letter at all. It was a page of signatures. His signature: Lee R. Blaise, it said, up and down several rows. No more a Blais, that quiet little burp of a name between "blay" and "bligh" that I couldn't pronounce anyway.

"Lee Blaise," I said to myself. Yes, yes. Clark Blaise. It looked right. It balanced. It was anchored.

PENGUIN · SHORT · FICTION

Other Titles In This Series

The Day is Dark/Three Travellers
Marie-Claire Blais

Café le Dog
Matt Cohen

High Spirits
Robertson Davies

The Pool In the Desert
Sara Jeannette Duncan

The Tattooed Woman
Marian Engel

Dinner Along the Amazon
Timothy Findley

Fables of Brunswick Avenue
Katherine Govier

Penguin Book of Canadian Short Stories
edited by Wayne Grady

Treasure Island
Jean Howarth

PENGUIN · SHORT · FICTION

Other Titles In This Series

The Moccasin Telegraph and Other Stories
W.P. Kinsella

The Thrill of the Grass
W.P. Kinsella

Champagne Barn
Norman Levine

Dark Arrows: Chronicles of Revenge
edited by Alberto Manguel

Darkness
Bharati Mukherjee

The Street
Mordecai Richler

Melancholy Elephants
Spider Robinson

The Light in the Piazza
Elizabeth Spencer

Also by Clark Blaise . . .

LUSTS

A hopeful young writer, Richard Durgin anticipates a life of fame, fortune, and romance when he meets the brilliant young poet Rachel Isaacs. Fatally attracted to each other, Richard and Rachel embark on a stormy marriage, and Rachel begins her meteoric rise as the creator of tortured poems of despair and isolation. Haunted by her past, unable to deal with the banality of American society, Rachel commits suicide, leaving Richard a legacy of mourning and guilt.

Lusts is the moving, perceptive story of Richard's search for redemption. As he pieces together recollections of his own life in the 1950s and 1960s with the frail threads of Rachel's life, Richard begins to come to terms with the "truth" of Rachel's reality and his own dreams and ambitions.

"On any and all of its many levels *Lusts* is a masterful work by an author of immense talent and insight."
— *Cleveland Plain Dealer*

"Clark Blaise is a born storyteller and an easy writer to like, to savor."
— *The New York Times Book Review*

"*Lusts* is a fine, rich novel, and it seems that the laurel is now in order for Clark Blaise."
— *Toronto Star*

"This is fiction doing what it should do."
— *Alice Munro*